A LONG

D0618854

Ann Turnbull was born in Hertford in 1943 and brought up in south east London. She has always loved books and knew from the age of ten that she wanted to be a writer. Her first book, *The Frightened Forest*, was published in 1974, since when she has written numerous stories for young people. These include *Pigeon Summer*, *No Friend of Mine* and *Room for a Stranger* – a trilogy about the Dyer family, set in the first half of the twentieth century in Shropshire, where she now lives with her husband and two cats. The first book, *Pigeon Summer*, was shortlisted for both the Smarties Book Prize and the W H Smith Mind Boggling Books Award and was televised on Channel Four. Ann Turnbull has two grown-up children.

Books by the same author

Friends and Foes Trilogy:
Pigeon Summer
No Friend of Mine
Room for a Stranger

Summer of the Cats

Trouble with Bats

A LONG WAY HOME

ANN TURNBULL

WALKER BOOKS
AND SUBSIDIARIES
LONDON • BOSTON • SYDNEY

For my family – all of them,
near and far

First published 1997 by Walker Books Ltd
87 Vauxhall Walk, London SE11 5HJ

This edition published 1998

2 4 6 8 10 9 7 5 3 1

Text © 1997 Ann Turnbull
Cover illustration © 1997 Jean-Paul Tibbles

The right of Ann Turnbull to be identified as author of
this work has been asserted by her in accordance with the
Copyright, Designs and Patents Act 1988.

This book has been typeset in Sabon.

Printed in England

British Library Cataloguing in Publication Data
A catalogue reocrd for this book is
available from the British Library.

ISBN 0-7445-5496-9

CONTENTS

CHAPTER ONE

Helen lay awake, listening to the rattle of milk churns in the street below. She didn't want to get up; she was afraid of what might happen today. But already it was dawn, and she could see the familiar attic room with its bare boards and cracked washstand, the framed text on the wall: "I will lift up mine eyes unto the hills, from whence cometh my help."

Against the far wall her mother's bed was stripped to its iron frame, the mattress taken away to be fumigated.

Helen felt grief, like a stone, in her chest.

Today was Wednesday. Yesterday had been the day of the funeral. Mum had died the week before, on Friday: Friday the fourteenth of November 1930, at five in the morning.

And today Mrs Bradley wanted to see Helen. To discuss her future, she'd said.

Her future. What would Mrs Bradley do

with her? She would not want to keep her here.

Someone tapped at the door: Ada. A tentative knock. Everyone was gentle with Helen now; sympathetic, embarrassed. Ada had offered to let Helen sleep in her room – "we could make up a camp bed" – but Helen had said no, and sensed Ada's relief.

"Helen?" called Ada. "Time to get up."

The room was unheated. Helen dressed under the bedclothes, then went to the window and opened the curtains.

"I will lift up mine eyes unto the hills…"

She had always loved this view: a long view, skimming the rooftops, a view of sky and birds, and, in the distance, a green hill with what looked like a ruined castle on its summit.

When she was a little girl she'd thought that was where her father lived, on that green hill. Mum said he'd lived out in the country, on a farm below a hillfort, and Helen had thought the hillfort was the castle she could see. She knew now that a hillfort wasn't a castle at all, just banks and ditches of turf. And she knew that her father was dead.

"But you always knew," her mother had said. "I told you."

She had. But for Helen, at five, or six, or even seven, he had been both dead and alive: dead in the trenches of Normandy, and yet alive in her imagination on that green hill.

Sometimes Helen saw people on the hill, small as ants.

"We could go there," she'd said. "One Sunday."

But Mum didn't know where the hill was, or how to get there. Instead, they'd go to the park, or to a fair or a market. There was never much time. Mum still had to get breakfast and prepare a cold lunch for Ada to take up, even on her Sunday off.

I'll never go now, thought Helen.

She left the room and went down the five flights of lino-covered stairs to the basement. Ada was in the kitchen, stirring porridge. "You like porridge, don't you, Helen?"

It wasn't Ada's place to cook, but she and Jenny between them would have to do Mum's job as well as theirs until Mrs Bradley found a replacement.

Helen tried to eat, and couldn't.

At half past nine Mrs Bradley rang from the study.

"That's for you," said Ada.

She took Helen up the first flight of back stairs to the ground floor, and opened the door that led into the other part of the house – the part inhabited by her employers. On the servants' side the door was covered with green baize. Helen stroked the fuzzy material, remembering how she had liked the feel of it when she first came here as a five-year-old.

It was not often, since, that she had crossed this threshold, and she was intimidated by the soft carpets, the glossy paintwork, the gleaming knobs on the other side.

Ada approached one of the closed doors and knocked.

"Come in," Mrs Bradley answered.

Ada shunted Helen in ahead of her. "Helen, madam," she said, and went out, closing the door.

Helen had never been in the study before. Her swift glance took in the towering shelves of books – Mr Bradley was a magistrate – the mahogany desk, the chairs upholstered in dark brown leather, the brown velvet curtains. On a low table, incongruous in this room, she saw her mother's battered tin trunk with an old address label hanging from its handle. Until Monday, when Mr Hollis, the handyman, came to fetch it, that trunk had always stood in a corner of the attic bedroom.

Mrs Bradley was dressed in dark pleated silk and looked compassionate.

Helen said, "Good morning, madam." It came out as little more than a whisper.

Mrs Bradley's voice, on the other hand, was full and confident. "Helen, my dear! This is a very sad business."

"Yes," said Helen. She looked at the carpet, which had a swirling ivy-leaf pattern.

"Your mother was an excellent woman,

Helen. I never had cause for complaint in all the years she was here. She will be very much missed."

"Thank you, madam," whispered Helen.

"And you, my dear. I must admit that when your mother applied for the post and mentioned a child I was uneasy – Mr Bradley needing quiet and order for his work…"

Helen remembered her mother's continual anxiety: "Now, sit down, Helen, and read a book. Or do some crayoning. Don't go running about." "Don't *shout*, Helen." "Don't clomp up the stairs." She remembered being refused a penny whistle because "the noise might annoy Mr Bradley". At school she was hopeless at skipping and ball games; she had never learned because the Bradleys' garden was out-of-bounds and the grand street where they lived was not one where children played.

"But you have never been any trouble," Mrs Bradley said.

"Thank you, madam."

Mrs Bradley glanced at Mum's trunk. Her manner changed; she had the air of one about to embark on unpleasant business. "I have been going through your mother's papers, Helen. She left some money: enough to pay for the funeral, and three guineas over, which will come to you when you leave school. Your mother was brought up in Crosshouses Orphanage in Solihull; she was a foundling, and her parents were never traced. No doubt you knew this."

Helen did. Her mother had told her about the orphanage.

"So you have no relatives on your mother's side, and your father…" She looked embarrassed. "It appears that your mother was not married."

Helen did not reply. She supposed she had always known this, although it had never been put into words before.

"Of course," Mrs Bradley continued, "I was not entirely surprised: a woman with a young child, looking for a place in service, calling herself a widow… There are letters in the trunk from a man we must presume was your father."

"Johnny," said Helen. "He died in the war."

"Yes." She paused, and Helen remembered Mum telling her that Mrs Bradley's only son had died, too, in a battle on the Somme.

Mrs Bradley continued. "But no address. Army addresses, but no home address."

"He lived in the country, madam," said Helen. "On a farm."

"Do you know the name of the nearest town?"

Helen didn't. She knew her mother had told her, but she could not remember.

"You see, my dear, because your mother

was unmarried, even if we could trace relatives on your father's side, you would have no claim on them. They probably know nothing of your existence, and…"

They won't want to take in the illegitimate child of a servant girl, thought Helen.

"Mr Bradley and I feel that there is no alternative but to send you to an orphanage."

She had put Helen's worst fear into words.

Her feelings must have shown in her face, for Mrs Bradley went on quickly. "There is an excellent institution in Halesowen. I am assured that you will be well looked after there. You will have the company of other girls" (Helen inwardly cringed) "and will be taught plain sewing and cooking and basic hygiene so that you can find employment when you leave –"

"Can't I stay here?"

Mrs Bradley looked startled and displeased at the interruption, but Helen persisted, desperation making her bold. "Mum taught me a lot. I used to help her. I can clean and carry water and lay fires and wash up and clean boots and shoes –"

"My dear child, you are not a cook. It's a cook-housekeeper I require, not a maid. Besides, you are too young. Eleven, aren't you, or twelve?"

"Twelve, madam."

Mrs Bradley became brisk. She wanted this

interview over with. "You must go to the orphanage. I have already made arrangements. You will remain there until you are fourteen and then you will be equipped to find a place in service. When the time comes I shall be only too pleased to give you a character reference."

She smiled, and Helen saw that she was glad to have thought of something kind to say, to soften the blow.

She rang the bell, and Ada appeared. "Ada, ask Mr Hollis to take Mrs Smith's trunk back upstairs. I shall not be needing it again. Helen will be leaving us on Friday morning."

"Friday!" The exclamation was out before Helen could suppress it.

Ada left the room.

"I shall be interviewing cooks today and tomorrow," said Mrs Bradley. "There may be someone able to start on Friday, and I'm sure you would rather not be here..."

And you need the bedroom, Helen thought.

She was dismissed.

On the farther side of the green baize door she began to cry, silently, because she had been trained not to make a noise.

I won't go to the orphanage, she thought. I'll never go there. They can't make me.

CHAPTER TWO

But she knew they could.

She went upstairs to the attic room. It was hers till Friday. After that she would never be alone again. She'd sleep in a dormitory, eat in a hall, be marched to church on Sundays, be dressed identically to a horde of others. She'd have lessons with rough girls who would dislike her because she was quiet and timid, and she would never get away from them; they'd have all day and all night to torment her.

There was a knock at the door.

"I've brought your mum's trunk," said Mr Hollis.

He set it down in the corner, where the oblong of lighter-coloured floorboards showed him its place.

His glance at Helen was gentle. "I'm sorry they're sending you away, my wench."

Helen nodded, unable to speak.

When he had gone she sank down beside the trunk and beat her fists on it. She was angry – furiously, unreasonably angry with her mother for dying. They had all had the flu – even Mrs Bradley – but only Mum had died. How could she do that to me? Helen thought. How could she leave me like this?

She opened the trunk and looked at its few contents: a large brown envelope labelled ALICE SMITH, a bundle of letters tied up with string, an official-looking envelope with a British Forces seal, two photographs and Mum's purse.

Helen was familiar with all these things, though she had never read the letters. She hated the thought of Mrs Bradley handling Mum's property, reading her letters, judging her.

She looked at the two photographs. One was a snapshot: her parents on a canal tow-path, beside a lock. The other was a studio portrait of her father in his army uniform.

"You're like him," Mum had said.

He had a thin face, a scattering of freckles, light coloured eyes. ("Green, like yours," said Mum. "And he was tall. I didn't reach his shoulder.")

The brown envelope contained certificates, mostly from Crosshouses Orphanage: merit awards for needlework and handwriting, a reference describing Alice Smith, aged fourteen, as "honest, reliable and hardworking". There were birth certificates, too – Helen's and her mother's. She looked at Mum's: *Alice – found at St Saviour's Church, Solihull, on the twelfth of April 1896.* No parents – just a line where their names should have been. And no surname. When had she acquired the name Smith, Helen wondered, and who chose it?

The official-looking envelope from the army was addressed to Miss A. Smith at an address in Harborne, Birmingham. Helen had never looked inside it before, though she guessed what it must contain. She took out her mother's last few letters to Pte. J. E. Davies, returned unopened. With them was a telegram dated December 1917, five months before Helen was born. It regretted to inform Miss Smith that Pte. Davies was "missing, presumed killed in action".

Helen stared at the telegram.

Presumed killed.

That meant they weren't sure, didn't it? Mrs Bradley had used that word "presume". A small fuse of anger began burning in Helen as she remembered: "…a man we must presume was your father."

Missing. Presumed killed. It must mean they never found his body.

And she remembered, then, overhearing the women talking in the kitchen about someone whose husband had turned up years later after

17

losing his memory – it must have been in the war – and she'd found another man and wasn't at all pleased to see him.

Suppose her father were still alive?

Mum hadn't thought so. She'd told Helen he was dead. And Mrs Bradley had only talked about tracing his family.

Helen thought about that family, on their farm in the country, under the hillfort. *They* must know. *They* could tell her.

I have to find them, she thought – even if they don't want me. They're the only family I've got. I have to know.

She went to the window and looked out at her green hill. John's train home used to take him west of Birmingham, a long way west, Mum had said; and he had to change at some town that began with *H* … Hemsbury – that was it. But where next? Mum had mentioned it, Helen was sure: a two-word name like King's Heath or Selly Oak. She struggled to remember, but it wouldn't come.

That was how they came to meet, Mum had told her: because Johnny lived in such a remote place. He'd got forty-eight hours' leave and there hadn't been time to go home, so he'd stayed with a friend in Birmingham, and they'd gone to a dance and Mum was there. Philip: that was the friend's name; he was the one who took the snapshot. She'd forgotten she knew until this moment. What else might come back to her? The name of that little town must be somewhere in her memory.

The sound of voices brought her attention down to the street below: the baker's boy, Jack, on his bicycle, turning in to the side passage and calling to Jenny.

Helen couldn't see Jenny, but she imagined her standing on the back doorstep, arms hugged round her against the cold, giggling. Jack was popular with the girls. He teased them and made them laugh and had nicknames for everyone. Helen's was Mouse.

He was shouting goodbye now. She saw him swing out onto the drive. He's like a bird, she thought, flying along, free. He can go where he likes.

She watched his bicycle disappear from view behind the plane trees that bordered Hartland Road. Just out of sight was the junction with the main road into town. All the trams and buses stopped there: trams to Birmingham city centre, buses to Halesowen, Dudley, Solihull, Wolverhampton.

I could get on a tram, Helen thought. I could run away. I don't have to wait for them to take me to the orphanage. I could catch a tram to the station and then a train to Hemsbury and go and find my father's family – perhaps even find him.

She'd need money. She ran back to the trunk and looked in Mum's purse: sixpence, and a farthing caught in the crease at the side. She searched the trunk thoroughly, but there was no trace of the three guineas that Mrs Bradley had mentioned. No doubt Mrs Bradley had taken that out to give to the guardians of the orphanage so that Helen could have it when she was fourteen.

But I need it now, Helen thought.

She wanted to run to Mrs Bradley and demand the money, but that would be stupid. Mrs Bradley wouldn't allow her to leave.

Sixpence would take her to the city centre and leave a bit over for food. But she'd have no money for the train, and Mrs Bradley would have the police out looking for her and they'd arrest her and take her to the orphanage.

She had to have money. But how? Where could she get it?

The answer came. She'd work. She'd get a job as a kitchenmaid. It was easy.

Except that she was only twelve.

She was taller than average, perhaps, but slight, not a grown-up figure at all. Could she pass for fourteen? She looked at her face in the bit of mirror that Mum had fixed over the washstand. Her mouse-brown hair was cut in a bob and held back with hair-slides. She took out the slides and pulled the hair up behind her head and fixed it with two of Mum's hairpins. It wasn't very secure, but it did make her look older. And if she wore Mum's clothes...

They were hanging on the rail in the corner: two striped cotton dresses, two dark blue, and Mum's own blouse and skirt for time off. Helen took out the blouse; she had always loved its silky feel. It gave off a warm, talcum powder smell – the smell of Mum's body. She held it against her face and her eyes filled with tears.

But this was no good. She put the blouse away, and took down one of the striped dresses and tried it for length. It wasn't too bad – Mum had been small – and she could pull it in with the apron.

I can do it, she thought.

Not today; everyone was up and about. Tomorrow would be best: early – so early that even Jenny wouldn't be up, blackleading the stove before breakfast. It would be dark. No one would see her, and she'd be on a tram and away long before she was missed.

She started packing.

CHAPTER THREE

"Nasty," the fat woman on the next seat said breathily.

Helen assumed she was referring to the weather, and nodded. She didn't want to talk. She was still trembling, relieved at last to be safe on board the tram, moving away from Hartland Road.

It had been easy leaving the house – except for a tense moment when she wrestled with the bolts and keys on the back door – but she had not reckoned on the weather. She was drenched in minutes as she struggled with her two bulging bags along the dark street.

Now she felt damp patches across her shoulders and a cold trickle ran from her hair down the inside of her coat collar.

"Mind you," said the woman, "they give out fine for tomorrow."

Helen turned aside. The window was

steamed up, and she had no idea where she was. Her carrier bag – a brown paper one from Loxleys the Bakers – was beginning to tear, weakened by the rain. She wished she had not brought Mum's knitting. The needles poked up and it was too bulky – a cardigan for Helen, finished except for the button band. It had been so hard to leave things behind – she thought of Ada going through Mum's possessions: the nightdresses and shoes, the romantic novels, *Red Letter* magazines, even her best skirt and blouse – but the trunk would have been impossible to manage; instead she had packed as much as possible in Mum's shopping bag and the carrier.

Nearly everyone on the tram seemed to be going to work. There was gossip and chatter all around her. In the seat in front two young women were sharing a hand mirror and putting on lipstick. The air smelt of wet gabardine and cigarette smoke.

The tram halted. More people got on, and had to stand. Helen saw the conductor approaching her with his ticket machine.

"Snow Hill, please," she said.

"That'll be threepence, miss."

He gave her a ticket and a threepenny bit change. She now had threepence farthing left. She thought of breakfast.

By the time the tram reached the city centre it was crammed with people. Cigarette ash

23

dropped on Helen's coat and loud, cheerful voices surrounded her. She felt isolated – not part of this friendly throng going to work.

"Snow Hill!" the conductor sang out.

The railway station. That was Helen's stop. She had to find out how much her ticket would cost. Grasping her bags she struggled down the aisle between the standing passengers.

The railway station was vast, an echoing vault full of voices and the rush of steam. Helen moved through the crowds. She saw a porter and asked, "Please, how much is a ticket to Hemsbury?"

"You want the ticket office, love. Over there."

Helen joined a queue at one of the booths. The clerk inside looked irritable. She hoped he wouldn't be angry if she didn't buy a ticket.

But the man was indifferent. "Third class single would be five and fourpence."

"Thank you."

Five and fourpence: less than a week's wages, if she was lucky. She could be in Hemsbury in a week. And, once there, she thought, perhaps she would remember the name of the place where her father's family lived, or find some clue to lead her to it.

But first she had to earn the five and fourpence. She knew that the place to look for jobs was *The Birmingham Post*, which cost a penny. She bought a copy from the newsagent's stall on the platform and stuffed it down the side of the shopping bag. Then she turned her attention to food.

There was a café across the platform. The smells of bacon and coffee came to her as she went in and found a table. She read the menu: sausages ... bacon ... fried eggs ... fried bread...

But she only had twopence farthing left.

She spent twopence on a cup of tea and half a slice of fried bread, and turned to the job advertisements page in *The Birmingham Post*.

There were plenty of jobs: maid of all work, live-in maid, kitchen-maid. But most of them had box numbers. You had to write, and give references. They were no good to Helen. No one would give her a reference, and she had to find somewhere today, or go back to Hartland Road.

Running her finger down the column, she came to one that gave an address: 16 Spring Crescent, Edgbaston. A kitchen maid. Write, giving references.

I'll go there, she thought. Maybe they won't mind me not writing, and if I look respectable perhaps they'll take me without a reference. Ada says people are desperate for servants these days.

Outside the station she found a city map on a board with YOU ARE HERE on it, and lists of streets at the side. She soon found Spring

Crescent and worked out how to get there, memorizing the names of the main roads.

On the map it hadn't looked far, but it took her half an hour to reach Edgbaston. The heavy bags pulled at her shoulders and the string handles of the carrier cut into her hand. She stopped often to change sides, and twice she had to ask the way. It frightened her to do this, but no one seemed interested in her. Yet she must have been missed by now at the Bradleys'. What would they do? she wondered. Would they call the police? They couldn't just let her go – not with Mr Bradley being a magistrate. When she saw a policeman in the distance she slipped down a side road and asked a delivery boy the way to Spring Crescent.

It was the next turning: a grand, tree-lined semicircle of Victorian houses that reminded her of Hartland Road. Number sixteen had a green front door with gleaming brass knocker and well-whitened steps. Keeping it that way would be her responsibility, she thought, if she got the job.

Now that she was here she felt nervous. She approached the basement steps and looked down. The door was closed, and she was afraid to go and knock on it.

As she stood hesitating, the door opened and a girl in cap and apron came out and emptied a pail of water into the drain. She straightened up, and saw Helen.

"Please," said Helen, "I've come about the job. Kitchen maid."

Her voice sounded small and young, and she wondered if they'd know at once that she was only a schoolgirl and send her away. But the maid just said, "Come down," and went back inside and called someone.

As Helen reached the bottom of the steps a woman came out, evidently the cook.

"What's your name?"

"Helen Smith."

The woman looked puzzled. "Did you have an appointment?"

"No … but I saw the job in the paper, and I thought…"

"Oh, you have to write in." She turned away. "Write in, and give references. Then they might see you."

"But I need somewhere now…"

The woman flicked a glance at Helen's bags. "The mistress won't see anyone off the street." And she closed the door in Helen's face.

Helen found that she was trembling. She felt humiliated and frightened. She should never have come, never have left Hartland Road. She would not get a place this way – she saw that now.

And yet she had to try. The thought of going back and facing Mrs Bradley was too awful.

She climbed the steps and went on, farther

round the crescent. When she was out of sight of number sixteen she tried another house. She knocked at the tradesmen's door and spoke to the housekeeper. This woman was kind, though there were no jobs.

"But if you've got nowhere to go, dear, there's a hostel in Church Lane—"

"It's all right. Thank you," said Helen, retreating in panic. "Hostel" sounded too much like "orphanage".

After a third house had refused her, she moved on. About a mile away she found herself in a less prosperous district, where the houses were narrower, with smaller gardens and shabbier paintwork. She walked up a long street. The bags pulled on her arms, and she was hungry and desperately tired. She thought of Hartland Road, the warm kitchen, Jenny making tea. In the nearby houses lights were coming on. It must be three o'clock at least. She'd been wandering about for hours.

A woman came out of a gateway, pushing a baby in a pram. Helen asked her if she knew of any jobs.

Nothing. But, "Have you tried the newsagents?" the woman asked. "They have cards in the window."

It was a ten minute walk to the shopping parade. Helen arrived exhausted. She felt that she could not walk another step. The fear was growing in her, minute by minute, that she would have to go back and face Mrs Bradley. It had begun to rain again, and the sky seemed to be darkening already towards a winter dusk. The lights in the shops glowed invitingly.

Outside a man muffled in a scarf and cap was selling chestnuts from a brazier of red-hot coals. They were a halfpenny a quarter.

"Can I have two ounces?" she asked.

The man wore fingerless gloves. He picked up a paper bag and growled, "Halfpenny a bag. Can't weigh them."

"I've only got a farthing," said Helen.

The man glanced at Helen, shrugged, and filled the bag a little over half full. "Two ounces," he said.

Helen gave him her last farthing.

She put the bags down and stood on the street corner eating. The hot skins cracked and burned her fingers, but the insides were worth it: warm, crumbly and filling.

She ate them all, then folded the bag and put it in her coat pocket. She saw the cards in the newsagent's window.

At first she thought there was nothing there, but then, amongst the offers of dressmaking and shoe repairs and second-hand prams, she saw what she was looking for:

Girl wanted, to live in. Must be strong. Apply inside.

She went into the shop.

"It's Mrs Grice," the woman said. She wrote the name and address on a piece of paper for Helen and told her how to get there. "She's a bit of a slave driver. Never keeps her girls."

"I don't want the job for long," said Helen.

"Well ... mind you stick up for yourself."

Helen felt apprehensive, but she picked up her bags and walked round the corner to 25 Mason Road. In a street of run-down houses, number twenty-five looked as if it were struggling to maintain respectability. The paintwork was peeling but there were net curtains at all the windows and the step was white.

Helen went to the tradesmen's entrance at the side, and as she did so one of the string handles of her carrier bag ripped through the damp paper and came away; the bag lurched open, and she had to clutch at her belongings and hold the bag against her hip as she knocked at the door.

An old woman answered her knock. She was heavy, with a lardy face and dark eyes like currants. Her expression was sour. Helen disliked her instantly. But I'm here now, she thought. She explained.

The woman looked her up and down. "What's your name?"

"Helen Smith."

"Age?"

"Fourteen."

"Fourteen?" The woman's expression didn't change.

"Yes." Helen was sure Mrs Grice didn't believe her.

"I've been two weeks without a girl. The last one went off with never a word – left us in the lurch." She looked at Helen's bags. A dress was escaping from the carrier; it was obvious that it contained all her belongings.

"I could start today," said Helen.

Mrs Grice nodded. "Five and six a week. Hours six in the morning to nine-thirty at night. Half-day Wednesday."

Helen knew it wasn't enough money. She didn't like Mrs Grice – didn't like the feel of the place. But she couldn't argue, with the winter evening coming on, cold and hungry as she was, and clutching her torn carrier bag.

"Thank you," she said, and followed the woman inside.

CHAPTER FOUR

"I do the cooking," said Mrs Grice, and Helen felt relief. "The larder is kept locked. I know you girls." She turned accusing eyes on her, as if Helen had already made plans to steal the biscuits. "Anything you need, you've to ask me."

A dark tiled corridor had brought them to the kitchen. There was a black range, a scrubbed wooden table, a stone-flagged floor. Smells of bread and bacon made Helen aware of how hungry she was. Mrs Grice showed her the broom cupboard, the scullery, the lean-to where the washtub and mangle were kept, the outside toilet; and as they went round she detailed Helen's duties: all the rugs to be taken up and beaten once a week, the chamber-pots to be emptied, washing to be done on Monday...

Back inside, Helen was taken into the living-room, where an old man sat beside the fire. He had watery blue eyes, red-rimmed, and yellowing whiskers.

"This is the new maid – Ellen," said Mrs Grice.

"Helen," said Helen, but if Mrs Grice heard, she ignored her.

Her husband turned his watery gaze on Helen, and winked.

It was a mere hint of a wink – too small for Mrs Grice to notice. Helen felt uneasy. What did it mean? "She's an old bag – don't mind her" … or something else? She took a step backwards.

"You'd better take your coat off," said Mrs Grice. "Hang it out there, in the hall."

Helen did so, though she felt unwilling; it was as if by that act she was committed to staying in this house.

Both living-room and dining-room had fires to be swept and laid, and so did the bedrooms.

Helen's room was one floor up from the Grices'. It contained a bed, a chair and a table with a jug and washstand.

Helen put her bags down.

She was aware of Mrs Grice sizing her up, arms folded across her chest. "You don't look very big." Helen wondered again if the woman realized she was under fourteen, if she'd change her mind about employing her. But Mrs Grice only said, "You'll need to be strong. I asked for a strong girl. There's the coal to carry, and the water. We haven't got electricity – can't afford it. I expect you're like all these young people – lights on and off all the time. There are gas lamps in most of the rooms, but in here you'll make do with a candle: one a week. I don't want you reading in bed, wasting my money."

They went back down to the main bedroom. Mrs Grice glanced at the bed. "Those sheets need changing. You can do that now." She turned as if to go.

"Mrs Grice?" Helen was frightened but determined. "Can I – can I have a drink first? And some food? I haven't…"

Mrs Grice put her hands on her hips. "So you're planning to eat me out of house and home before you've done a hand's turn, are you?"

But she ordered Helen downstairs, unlocked the pantry door with much jangling of keys, and cut two slices of bread. These she put on the table with a bowl of dripping. She took out a twist of paper containing tea leaves: "That's *your* tea. It's to last you the week."

"Thank you," said Helen.

"When you've changed those sheets you can unpack your bags and make up your own bed. Mr Grice and I will want a pot of tea in the living-room at four o'clock." She showed Helen where the china was kept. "At six o'clock you can bring us our dinner. There's a stew in the oven, and some jelly and custard in the larder. I'll get that out later. Have you got an afternoon dress?"

"Yes. In my bag upstairs."

"Good. Well, get on. Don't waste time."

She was gone. Helen ran to the sink, poured herself a cup of water and gulped it down, refilled it and drank another, gasping in her eagerness. Then she put the kettle on and spread dripping on the bread and ate both slices. She sat alone in the kitchen, sipping the hot tea she had made. "A bit of a slave driver," the newsagent had said.

When she heard movement in the room above she jumped up, tipped away the remaining tea and washed the dishes, fearful that Mrs Grice would accuse her of slacking. She went back upstairs, pulled off the sheets from the bed and left it to air.

Her own room had a view of a concrete yard and a drainpipe. The sky was a long way off between high brick walls. Helen put on one of the dark afternoon dresses and a white apron. The dress was creased, but the apron hid most of it and pulled in the slack.

She hung her clothes on the two hooks on the back of the door and made up the bed. The sheets were old and thin. As she tucked the bottom one in she felt it rip. "Oh, no!" she exclaimed, and tears sprang to her eyes. Perhaps she could mend it before Mrs Grice found out; Mum had taught her how to do darning. But she'd have to find a needle and cotton. It was horrible, being in this strange house – not knowing where anything was. And the bed was horrible, too: no springs, only one blanket, and an eiderdown from which nearly all the feathers had escaped. She'd have to pile clothes on top of it.

She put her nightdress under the lumpy pillow and Mum's knitting on the floor. It was the knitting – so familiar and so out-of-place here, in this unfriendly house – that made her suddenly crumple and cry. She wanted Mum. She longed for her. She wanted Mum to come in now and put her arms round her and tell her it was all right, she could come home, she didn't have to stay with hard-hearted Mrs Grice and her strange husband, she could come home and have tea and go to bed in her attic room at Hartland Road, and everything would be the same as before.

She understood now why Mum had always said Mrs Bradley was a good employer, though she'd seemed to Helen remote and uninterested in them. At Mrs Bradley's a new maid would have been welcomed and given a proper meal and time to settle in; and, besides, there were other people there: Ada, and Jenny, and Mr Hollis. Here, Helen would be quite alone.

But it's only for a week, she told herself. She wiped her eyes and blew her nose. Mrs Grice would pay her five and six a week. Next Thursday – no, it would probably have to be Friday; Friday was usually pay-day – she could collect her five and six and leave this house and catch a train to Hemsbury.

She felt for the package of letters and photos at the bottom of her bag, and looked again at the photograph of her father in his army uniform. She felt sure that he was alive, that soon she would find him.

A bell rang below. She realized, with a start of alarm, that it must be four o'clock already and she had not made the tea. She put the photograph away and hid the package at the bottom of her bag, under her spare vest. Then she ran downstairs.

When she came into the living-room ten minutes later Mr and Mrs Grice were seated by the fire. Mrs Grice glanced at the clock before saying, "Thank you, Ellen."

Helen tried once more. "It's Helen, madam."

"Ellen, yes," said Mrs Grice. "That will be all."

Helen knew that Mrs Grice was not deaf. By ignoring her name she was saying, "Ellen was good enough for servant girls in my day and it'll be good enough for you. Don't you go giving yourself airs."

I hate her, Helen thought. But it won't be for long. Eight days. I can bear it for eight days.

CHAPTER FIVE

"I don't want any followers here," Mrs Grice said on that first morning as she boiled eggs for herself and her husband and allocated three slices of bread and dripping to Helen. "I had enough of that with the last girl."

Helen knew "followers" meant men friends; Mrs Bradley had waged war on them, too.

"I'm a bit young…" she started to say; then remembered that she was supposed to be fourteen. Perhaps fourteen was old enough.

"Oh, I know! You all pretend to be innocent," said Mrs Grice. "But I'll be watching you." She put the eggs on a tray. "When you've finished your breakfast you can make some toast and bring it in with the marmalade and butter."

Helen ate her bread and dripping. The marmalade glowed golden in its glass dish. Would Mrs Grice notice, she wondered, if she pinched a bit, just on the end of a teaspoon? She was too afraid of her to find out. She drank the tea, then made toast and took the tempting marmalade away to the dining-room.

Since getting up at five-thirty she had laid the fires, scrubbed the front step, polished the door knocker and blackleaded the kitchen stove. She had never done such heavy work before and already she was tired. But Mrs Grice had a two-week backlog for her to catch up on. All the downstairs mats were to be hung on the washing line and beaten, all the floors to be swept and the tiles washed.

The mats were heavy, the dining-room one so big that she could not lift it on her own, and Mrs Grice had to help her carry it outside and hang it up. When she thought she had finished beating it Mrs Grice came out and made her give it another whacking. "Put your back into it, girl," she said.

Helen's shoulders ached, and clouds of dust blew in her face and hair. She spent two hours lifting and beating mats. While she beat the last one Mr Grice passed by to use the outside toilet. When he came out he stood watching her. Helen wished he would go away. Something about the way he looked at her made her uneasy.

"Want to earn some money?" He was holding up a threepenny bit between thumb and forefinger.

Helen stopped beating.

"Get me some tobacco from the shop?" he asked.

Helen put down the carpet beater and approached him reluctantly.

"That's a good girl." He counted out coins with mottled, shaking hands. "A shilling. Gold Flake. And threepence for you." He put the money in her hand and closed her fingers over it. Helen shrank from his touch. As soon as she could, she darted away.

She was putting on her coat when Mrs Grice appeared. "And where do you think you're off to, miss?"

"Mr Grice asked me to buy him some tobacco."

"He can wait. You've got work to do. You ask me before you leave the house."

"Yes, madam."

Helen dusted and swept. She scrubbed the passages and kitchen floor on her hands and knees. By the time she tipped the cold, scummy water down the drain she was shaking with exhaustion.

Mrs Grice was cooking, making a meat pie. Glorious smells filled the kitchen.

"Your dinner's there," she said. "You'd better clean yourself up and have it, then you can go and do the master's errands."

Helen's dinner was warmed-up stew – the remains of her employers' dinner of the night before. For pudding there was a piece of fruit cake; it was stale, but she was too hungry to care.

Running to the shops in the rain, she felt free. Mrs Grice had allowed her ten minutes, and she savoured each one.

When she got back and gave him the tobacco, Mr Grice offered her a mint humbug.

"No, thank you, sir."

He chuckled. "You're a quiet one, Ellen. Not like the last girl! Little mouse, aren't you?" And he winked again.

Helen said nothing. "Mouse." Jack had called her that, and she hadn't minded; she'd rather liked it. But Jack was different.

She finished dusting the downstairs rooms; then she polished a heap of boots and shoes.

It was half past two. Her mother and the maids at Hartland Road had often had little to do in the afternoons. They'd read or knit and chat before the bell rang for tea.

She'd get out the photographs and letters, she decided. Perhaps something in the package would jog her memory. Then she'd know where she needed to make for after she'd got to Hemsbury.

But as soon as her hand touched the banister, Mrs Grice came out of the living-room like a spider from its lair. "Ellen! Have you dusted the bedrooms?"

Helen thought with despair of the Grices'

bedroom with its dark furniture and clutter of ornaments.

"I was just going to," she lied.

The black eyes saw through her, marked her down as sly. "Then you'd better take a duster, hadn't you?"

"Yes, madam."

"And did you turn out the cutlery tray and clean it?"

"There wasn't time."

"Well, there's time now. Off you go. And if you finish before half past three you can polish the silver. I don't want you idling."

Helen flicked the duster around the photographs and vases and bottles of pills in the Grices' bedroom. She was worn-out. And hungry. She thought of teatime at Hartland Road: Mum's scones and fresh bread and soft-boiled eggs.

If I'm dusting bedrooms, she thought, I can do my room, too, and sit down for a minute and look at those letters.

It was a mistake.

She woke, stiff, crouched on the floor with her head against the side of the bed. There was a sound: the ringing of the bell, far-off, insistent. Then Mrs Grice's voice in the stairwell: "Ellen!"

She stepped out, groggy with sleep.

Mrs Grice stood below her, on the first landing. "It's four o'clock," she said.

"I'm coming, madam. Sorry," said Helen.

"And where were you?"

"I fell asleep."

"You don't fall asleep if you stay on your feet."

"No, madam."

"Reading a magazine in my time, no doubt."

"I wasn't—"

"I don't allow magazines in this house. Giving girls ideas. If I find anything of that sort, there'll be trouble."

The word "find" scared Helen. Would Mrs Grice search her room?

"I've put the kettle on," said Mrs Grice. "You'd better come down and make tea."

Tea for the Grices was served with scones. Helen hoped she might get a scone with her own tea, but there was none. And when her supper came at six it was bread and margarine with a trace of jam. It didn't satisfy her. She longed for another slice of bread, but Mrs Grice had locked the pantry.

She served dinner, washed up, dried the dishes, took coal to the bedrooms and, later, hot water. It was nine-thirty before she had filled the last hot-water bottle and was free to go to her room. Once there, she lit the candle and – thinking of Mr Grice – wedged the chair under the door knob. Then she undressed and went straight to bed. She wouldn't have dared waste the candle stub reading Mum's letters now, even if she'd had the energy.

"I need you to come shopping with me, Ellen," Mrs Grice said on Saturday morning. "I don't have anything delivered – don't trust these tradesmen; they'll fob you off with any old stuff."

She must have seen the disappointment in Helen's face, for she added, "Yes, I expect you were hoping to chat to all the boys on the doorstep. Well, you won't get the chance here. Fetch the bags; they're in the cupboard."

Helen thought she would never be able to carry the shopping. Her shoulders were stiff and painful; that was the rug-bashing. She had slept heavily, and still felt half-asleep, but the fresh air revived her. The streets, the people, the sounds of birds and traffic reminded her that there was a world outside 25 Mason Road. She saw a tram that went to the city centre, and noted where it stopped. Soon, she thought. Next Friday.

Monday was washday, and even though she and Mrs Grice did the washing together, Helen was so tired by Tuesday morning that she felt she would never survive until Friday. She had not told Mrs Grice she planned to leave, but on Tuesday afternoon, when she was sent out to post a letter, she took the threepenny bit Mr Grice had given her and bought a newspaper. That night, for the first time, she burned the candle and forced herself to stay awake and read through the "Situations Vacant". She knew she had to have a job in service, even if it was only for a day or two, while she searched for the name of the place after Hemsbury. Without one she'd have nowhere to live.

There were only two suitable positions in Hemsbury: one for a lady's companion, the other for a kitchen maid at a hotel. Both wanted a written application. She'd need writing paper, a pen, an envelope, and a stamp. The twopence in her pocket would not pay for all that.

I'll have to just go, she thought; give notice, and go, and get on a train.

On Friday morning she waited for Mrs Grice to hand her a pay packet, but nothing was offered. At dinner-time she summoned her courage and asked, "Could I have my money now, Mrs Grice?"

Mrs Grice frowned. "Money? What do you want money for?"

"My wages..." Helen faltered.

"Your wages!" Mrs Grice looked outraged. "You'll get your wages at the end of the month, like everyone else. You don't expect me to hand out money every week for you to fritter away?"

Helen was too stunned to reply. Of course. She should have known. Servants were always paid monthly. Mum was. Jenny was. She'd become so obsessed with earning the train fare she'd forgotten that. She felt distraught. It was impossible to imagine enduring another three weeks here. She had been keyed up, ready to accept her money, to say, "I'm leaving, madam." Now she felt as if the door of a prison had been shut in her face.

I can't stay here for a month, she thought. I'll have to get away.

CHAPTER SIX

"Do you want a paper today, sir?"

Helen had forced herself to approach Mr Grice. She hated doing it, but she was hungry.

Mr Grice patted her hand. "You're a good girl, Ellen. Here – " he gave her the money, and a penny over – "get yourself a cake, eh? You could do with putting on a bit of weight." He eyed her waistline.

Helen moved away. Mr Grice frightened her, and she knew she must make sure she was never alone with him. She was always alert, as she worked, for the smell of his tobacco or the shuffle of his slippered feet. The house was probably safe enough, she thought, with Mrs Grice watching and listening, but going to the outside toilet was an ordeal, especially after dark.

She put the money in her apron pocket. If only she could keep the penny, she thought, and hide it with the other small change in the sock at the bottom of Mum's bag. But she had long since given up trying to do that.

At first she had been determined to save the train fare to Hemsbury so that she could leave before her month was up. She soon realized that Mr Grice would pay her to fetch his tobacco and papers and she took advantage of it. There should have been several shillings in the sock, but now, after two weeks, there was only fourpence.

It was the hunger that defeated her. All she could think about was food. There was a baker's shop next door to the newsagent's, and nearly all her pennies were spent there, on buns and scones, and bread rolls reduced at the end of the day.

Mrs Bryant at the baker's got to know her. One day Mrs Grice gave Helen a shilling and sent her out for Eccles cakes. They were cheaper than expected.

Mrs Bryant winked. "I'll put an extra one in for you, shall I? She won't know."

A few weeks ago Helen would have been shocked; it would never have occurred to her not to take her employer the change. Now her only decision was whether to keep it or have an Eccles cake for herself. She chose the cake.

She had given up hope, at last, of getting away before the end of the month. Hunger and exhaustion kept her chained to Mrs Grice. At night she fell instantly asleep. Her half-day off could only begin when she had finished her usual chores, and she spent the few hours that were left sleeping.

She had not looked at the letters. She had no time or energy, and there seemed little point, anyway, while she was trapped at Mason Road. Mrs Grice made sure she was never idle. "Whenever you have a spare moment, Ellen, there's mending to be done. Fetch me that basket; I'll show you."

So while she drank her tea in the afternoon Helen would repair the seam of a pillowcase or thread new elastic through the casing of Mrs Grice's baggy pink drawers.

"You want to give in your notice," Mrs Bryant advised when Helen came in that day and chose a bun. "Get a place where they feed you better. You're as thin as a rake. She's taking advantage."

"I'm all right," said Helen. She was afraid that Mrs Grice would refuse to pay her if she tried to leave. The woman had probably guessed she was under fourteen and had no one to turn to. Somehow she'd have to survive till the end of the month.

"Here, take a roll, too," said Mrs Bryant. "Go on. They'll be stale by tomorrow, any road."

"Thank you," said Helen.

*   *   *

That was on Thursday. On Saturday Mrs Grice caught a cold and couldn't go shopping. Instead she sent Helen. She gave her a list and counted out the money down to the last penny. "And no hanging about the street. You come straight back."

Helen did. She also made up a cough medicine to Mrs Grice's instructions, and stirred it on the stove until it was blended. Mrs Grice sat by the fire, shivering and heavy-eyed, and sipped it.

"You'd best take to your bed, woman," said her husband, sneaking a glance at Helen.

Helen tensed. But to her relief Mrs Grice refused. "Take to my bed? I've got too much work to do. You can fetch me a shawl, Ellen. I'll be out and about in a day or two."

But on Tuesday there was a cold wind blowing, and flurries of sleet, and Mrs Grice decided to send Helen shopping again. Once more she gave her the exact money: seven shillings and tenpence halfpenny. It was a longer list this time; she was beginning to trust Helen.

Helen looked at the money. Nearly eight shillings. Less than her due wages – much less – but more than enough to get her to Hemsbury. She didn't hesitate for long. It wasn't stealing, she decided; not really.

Mrs Grice's cold had made her deaf. Helen managed to run upstairs without her hearing and stuff things quickly into her own bag and Mrs Grice's shopping bag. She piled them in: clothes, books, knitting, and the precious papers pushed well down. Her exhaustion lifted; energy and hope had returned.

She crept downstairs with the bulging bags. Her heart beat fast. If Mrs Grice opened the living-room door now she'd catch her, and then what would she do? Call the police, most like. But Helen was desperate. She seized her coat and scuttled into the kitchen.

As she thrust her arms into the coat sleeves she heard shuffling footsteps along the passage. Mr Grice's voice quavered, "Ellen...?"

He came into the room. Her hand was on the door knob. He glanced at the bags. "Ellen? You're not –" He turned and called over his shoulder, "Polly! You'd better come! Ellen's away!"

With a gasp of fear Helen seized the bags, darted out, and slammed the door behind her. She ran down the road, the bags bumping against her legs. She wasn't afraid of Mr Grice; he was doddery. But suddenly she heard a yell behind her, and there was *Mrs* Grice, flapping down the road in her slippers, shaking her fist and screeching, "Stop her! Stop thief! She's stolen my money! Stop her!"

Doors opened. A woman turned and stared. Some boys began to run. Helen was terrified. Fear gave her speed, and she raced away, outpacing the boys: down the road, round the corner, over the crossing – and there was the tram, the tram that said CITY CENTRE on the front, approaching its stop! Gasping for breath she ran the last few yards, reached it, and sprang on board.

The tram pulled away. She was free.

CHAPTER SEVEN

Helen sat in an empty compartment on the train to Hemsbury. She heard doors slamming, shouted goodbyes, all the clamour of the big station. But she didn't look out. She sat still and tense, her ticket clutched in her hand. One bag was tucked between her knees on the floor, the other on the seat beside her. All the way here, on the tram, in the city centre, at the ticket office, she had been in terror of a policeman approaching her, alerted by the angry Grices. She could hardly believe what she had done: taken Mrs Grice's money *and* her shopping bag; she imagined her description circulated to the police, station staff on the look-out. She had chosen the empty compartment deliberately. She would not feel safe until she had left Birmingham.

At last the whistle blew. The train steamed out of the station. As it gathered speed Helen let her fears go; her breathing slowed down. For a while she leaned back and gazed out at the view of rooftops, narrow brick houses, backyards and washing lines, and let the rhythm of the train lull her; then she fell asleep.

When she woke there was someone else in the compartment: a woman who had spread herself and her belongings comfortably across the space opposite, her coat tossed back, shopping bags, gloves and hat on the surrounding seats. She had dark, untidy hair and a friendly smile.

Helen, in sudden panic, looked out of the window and saw fields, hedges, more fields... Where was she? Had she missed her station?

"Don't worry," the woman said. "We're not at Wraybury yet." Helen's alarm subsided. "You're going to Hemsbury, aren't you? Same as me."

Helen nodded, then remembered, with another start, the ticket she'd been holding – but it lay on top of the bag beside her.

"You dropped your ticket," the woman said. "I found it on the floor. I showed it to the ticket inspector when he came round. We didn't have the heart to wake you – you looked so peaceful."

Helen found her voice. "Thank you." She yawned.

"I think you needed a good sleep," the woman said.

She's curious about me, Helen thought. She wondered if the woman had noticed what was in her bags: a striped maid's dress lay folded at the top of one; in the other the knitting needles poked up, and a copy of *Heidi*.

"Going to stay in Hemsbury, are you?" the woman asked.

She knows I've got a one-way ticket, Helen thought. "Yes," she said.

"It's a nice town," the woman said. "I've lived there nine years now. Since I married. I come from Oswestry. Are you staying with relations?"

"I'm looking for work," said Helen.

"In service?"

"Yes."

"I thought that was a maid's uniform. Though you hardly look old enough to be out at work."

"I'm fourteen."

"That's what I thought. I said to myself, 'Well, she's no more than fourteen, and all on her own.' You're a Brummie, aren't you? I can tell from your accent. What brings you to Hemsbury? There must be more jobs in the city – *and* better pay."

Helen felt hunted. The woman was kind and interested, but she was the sort that just wouldn't leave people alone. She'd been sitting there while Helen slept, watching and wondering. "I ... felt like a change ... the country..." Helen said.

The woman laughed. "I wouldn't call Hemsbury the country! But perhaps it is – compared with Birmingham. You've got a place to go to, I suppose – living-in?"

Helen felt herself turning pink. "No. I'm going to look when I get there."

The woman seemed shocked. "What will you do if you don't find somewhere? Where will you sleep? A young girl like you shouldn't be looking for work in a strange town on her own." She looked at Helen through narrowed eyes. "Have you run away from home?"

This was worse even than Helen had feared. She'd be found out; sent back to the Grices. She said nothing.

"You have, haven't you? Does your mother know where you are?"

"My mother's dead," said Helen, and was glad to see the woman's embarrassment. "I'm an orphan."

"I'm sorry about that. So it's your job you've left – your place in service?" Once again she looked closely at Helen. She lowered her voice. "You're not in trouble, are you?"

Helen knew what that meant. She blushed. "No!" She could see that the woman was uncertain whether to believe her, and she rushed on. "I ran away because they were cruel to me! They worked me too hard. And there wasn't enough to eat. And they were horrible. And they said I had to stay till the end of the month but I … I just couldn't bear it."

Her eyes filled with tears, and she turned away towards the window, and saw Wraybury Station coming into view.

Perhaps someone will get in, she thought, and then this conversation will stop.

But no one did.

"When did you last eat?" The woman was rummaging in one of her many bags.

"Seven o'clock." Helen realized how hungry she was.

The woman had produced a paper bag that smelled enticingly of fresh baking and sugar. "Have a doughnut."

When Helen began to shake her head, she insisted. "Go on. I bought them for my children, but there are plenty here."

The doughnut was the nicest thing Helen had eaten since she left Hartland Road: fresh, still warm, frosted with sugar, and with a generous filling of damson jam that oozed out when she bit into it. She ate slowly, prolonging the pleasure, then sighed and licked sugar from her fingers, one by one.

The woman smiled. Her next question surprised Helen. "Do you like children? Little ones?"

"I don't know," said Helen.

The woman laughed. "Well, that's honest! I've got two, Irene and Dennis. Irene's six and

Dennis is just a baby – he was a year old on August Bank Holiday. I'm sure you'd like them." She leaned forward. "You see, I'm looking for a maid myself. Just a young girl straight from school to help out. I've seen a couple but haven't got suited yet. My last girl, Amy, was from the country; she got homesick."

When Helen did not reply, she continued, "Of course, I can't pay city wages, but the work isn't heavy. Six and eight a week, with a half day and every Sunday off. Mrs Petty is my name. My husband's the manager of Stillwell's the Chemist's. We live near the centre of town. What do you think?"

"Mrs Grice won't give me a character," said Helen.

"Because you ran away? That doesn't matter. I'll take you on trust. You look a decent girl to me."

Helen wished it were true. She had not felt decent since she had taken Mrs Grice's money, but she couldn't bring herself to tell Mrs Petty about that.

"They'll be surprised," Mrs Petty laughed, "if I come back from Christmas shopping in Wolverhampton with a new maid! You will come, won't you?"

"Yes," said Helen. "Please."

CHAPTER EIGHT

"Buppy!" roared Dennis.

He sat in his highchair, banging a spoon on the tray in mounting excitement as Mrs Petty cut up his bread and butter into fingers.

Helen watched. This would be *her* job. How would she ever cope? She had thought babies were tiny, passive creatures, but feeding Dennis was like fuelling a locomotive.

Irene nibbled at a slice of bread. "*Wait, Dennis. It's coming!*" She giggled, turning dark eyes on Helen. "He's naughty, isn't he?"

Irene had been chattering to Helen ever since they met, an hour ago: about her family, her school, Tibby the cat, her doll Marian. Now she said, "I've got a wobbly tooth – look!"

"Not at the table, Irene," said Mrs Petty. She turned to Helen. "Eat up. There's plenty here."

But Helen was too nervous to eat much. Mrs Petty saw this and said, "You can have some more later, when the children are out of the way." She explained to Helen where everything was kept and what she would be expected to do. Helen began to realize that her new employer wanted a girl who was as much nursemaid as kitchen-maid.

The children were stickily absorbed with their doughnuts when they all heard the front door opening.

"Daddy!" exclaimed Irene. Dennis yodelled, waving his spoon.

Irene was down from her chair and running into the passage before Mrs Petty could stop her. "Daddy, we've got a surprise!" Her mother followed. There was laughter, explanation. Helen heard the man's voice – caught the word "references". Her stomach tightened. Perhaps she wouldn't be able to stay, after all.

But when Mr Petty came in, he was smiling. He greeted her formally, shook hands, said he hoped she'd suit. Then he planted a kiss on Dennis' head and retreated with his newspaper. Helen guessed he would not see the children again until they were cleaned up, ready for bed.

When tea was over Dennis lolled in his chair, blissfully smeared with jam. An explosion of crumbs littered the room. Helen was worried by so much disorder. She retrieved a sticky spoon from the floor and began clearing the table.

"Leave that, Helen," said Mrs Petty, who seemed unconcerned at the chaos. "You go upstairs and settle in. Have an hour or so to yourself before we put these two to bed. I'll ring when I need you."

Irene attached herself to Helen. "Can I go too?"

"No," said her mother. "Helen's room is private."

Helen was grateful for that. She made her escape.

It was the usual attic room, bare and simple. But the view was better than at Mason Road. She could see the back garden with its lawn and bird-bath, beyond that the spires and rooftops of Hemsbury and, in the distance, hills.

She unpacked quickly and put her clothes away. At the bottom of Mrs Grice's shopping bag was the parcel of letters. Now, for the first time in nearly three weeks, she had the opportunity to read them and search for clues.

She settled herself on the bed and took out the first bundle: her mother's letters – the last few, which Johnny had never received. As she read, she realized that her mother had found writing difficult. The letters were short, laboured, the handwriting round and careful; they didn't have the sound of Mum's voice.

She skimmed them and turned to the other package.

Johnny's were different: the handwriting looser, the letters longer and chattier. There were jokes, descriptions of long sea voyages, awful food, awful weather. There was soft lovey-dovey stuff as well – embarrassing; she didn't like reading it. And nothing about his home. She read on, hoping, but although he sometimes wrote of his childhood on the farm he never said where it was. She came to the end of the last one. Nothing.

Helen felt desperate. She'd expected so much of the letters, and they were of no help after all. Angry and disappointed, she stuffed the package away. She'd have to search elsewhere.

She went to the window again. Perhaps the ancient fort was on one of those hills. But how could she find out?

Maps. Maps had things marked on them. She remembered at school seeing a castle shown on a map in old-fashioned lettering.

The next day, when she found herself alone in the living-room, she put down her duster and looked along the rows of books in the glass-fronted cabinet. A few novels, a dressmaking book, *Dr Winstanley's Book of Child Management*, *The Gardener's Year* ... no maps. She tried the magazine rack, but that only contained back numbers of *Good Housekeeping* – and yesterday's newspaper, which it was her job to remove.

There was no time after that to think about where to search. Mrs Petty did the cooking, but Helen had to give the children their dinner and tea, and she ate with them, serving her employers separately. Around these events the cleaning was to be fitted in.

She soon found that mealtimes at the Pettys' were much more fun than at the Grices'. She was allowed the same food as the family, and plenty of it, and Irene helped her cope with Dennis.

Dennis had strong opinions but few words to express them. Irene interpreted for Helen: "He's gone quiet. That means he needs his nappy changed." "He's crying. He wants his rusk."

She observed Helen, too. Nothing Helen did escaped Irene's notice. She saw that Helen was nervous of Tibby; she noticed her accent and asked her why she called Dennis "the babby"; she asked her why her dresses were too big for her and why she didn't have a tin trunk like Amy's, and why she could read better than Amy although Amy was bigger.

She's another one like her mother, Helen thought: all questions. Mrs Petty had soon found out about Helen's past life, her mother's job, her illness and death. Helen had to be careful; there was a danger of responding to the friendly enquiries and letting something slip. She dared not reveal that she was only twelve; Mrs Petty would probably feel obliged to send her straight back to Birmingham.

On Thursday the paper boy delivered two newspapers: *The Times* and *The Hemsbury Chronicle*. Helen put them both, smoothed-out, on the desk in the living-room ready for Mr Petty when he came home from work. She thought nothing more about it until the next morning when she saw *The Hemsbury Chronicle* lying open on the settee. FARMING NEWS said the heading at the top of the page, and there was a drawing of a wintry field, and paragraphs headed WHISTLEY, CHURNFORD, TENTERBURY.

Place names. Places where farmers lived. She seized the paper and scanned through, looking for names with two words. She found one – Preston Norbury – but it meant nothing to her.

The door opened, and she started and dropped the paper as Mrs Petty came in.

"This won't get the work done, Helen!"

She was smiling, but Helen blushed, folded the paper, and muttered, "Sorry, madam. Just tidying."

She picked up her duster, but Mrs Petty said, "Never mind that now. Take the children to the park. It'll put roses in your cheeks – and give me a bit of peace."

Helen willingly obliged. They went out,

muffled in coats and scarves, Dennis in his pram, Irene skipping alongside. The wind, with hard specks of snow in it, whipped their faces. They had taken bread for the ducks on the lake, and Helen lifted Dennis out of the pram and held his reins while they fed them. The ducks waddled out of the water, quacking. "Hello!" said Dennis. "Hello! Hello! Hello!"

When two swans appeared he grew excited. "Duck! 'Nother duck!"

"Swans!" Irene corrected him.

The swans sailed close to the shore. Dennis struggled to reach them. "Duck!" he insisted, and grew red in the face as Helen held him back.

"We'd better put him in the pram again," she said.

Dennis thrashed and screamed as they left the park.

"He calls all birds 'duck'," said Irene when at last the lake was out of sight and Dennis had calmed down. "Even sparrows. And he calls dogs 'cat'!" She laughed, showing gappy front teeth.

They went a different way home, through the centre of town instead of round the walls. They passed Stillwell's the Chemists, where Mr Petty worked. The lamps were lit inside, and the light shone through the tall glass jars full of jewel-coloured liquid in the window: deep blue, crimson, emerald. Irene wanted to go in and say hello to her father, but Helen said no, better not. She was a little in awe of Mr Petty and, besides, she didn't want to risk unstrapping Dennis, who now lay tear-stained and exhausted with eyelids drooping. The Christmas lights swung and sparkled in the main streets, and Crawfords, the big department store, had a row of Christmas trees twinkling above the ground floor windows.

"I'm going to write a letter to Santa," said Irene.

Helen thought of last Christmas: the stocking at the end of her bed with an orange, an embroidered handkerchief and a rolled-up comic in it – Mum's doing. There would be nothing this year.

"What's the matter, Helen?" Irene was staring up at her, frowning.

Helen shook away the memory. "I'm lost. Which way do we go now?"

"Up there, past the library."

Helen looked at the massive stone building. PUBLIC LIBRARY, it said over the door. Lamps, hanging on chains from the ceiling, were visible through the high windows, but nothing else. She imagined all the shelves of books. Perhaps there were maps, too…

She went to the library on her afternoon off, the following Thursday. The hall was hushed, the quiet broken only by the occasional rustle of paper; notices on the walls demanded SILENCE. A few people sat at tables, reading, or moved, soft-footed and purposeful, between the tiers of shelves.

Helen crept around, glancing at titles. She could not see any maps. She'd have to ask.

One librarian was busy issuing books. The other was across the room, rearranging a card index. Helen went and stood near her. The woman was thin and forbidding in steel-rimmed glasses and reminded Helen of a teacher she had particularly disliked.

Either the librarian was unaware of Helen or she was deliberately ignoring her. Helen hovered, shifting her weight from one leg to the other. She didn't dare interrupt, and in any case she wasn't sure how to explain what she wanted.

Then a man came along, approached the librarian, and said, "Excuse me. I'm looking for some information on delftware," and the woman immediately left her work and set off, squeaky-soled, taking him to the far end of the library, where they remained in whispered consultation.

The other librarian now had a queue of people waiting.

Helen went out, into the December dusk.

I'll try again next week, she thought.

But she had forgotten Christmas. Thursday of the following week was Boxing Day, and

67

the library was closed, and even if it hadn't been she had far too much to do to think about looking for the hillfort.

The Pettys gave Helen a red woollen scarf and gloves for Christmas. Helen loved the bright colour. Mrs Bradley would never have given a maid anything like that. Mum had worked for Mrs Bradley for seven years and every Christmas she had received the same thing: a cotton dress length in either stripes or dark blue – a new uniform which she would have to pay a dressmaker to make up for her.

Mrs Petty treats me like a person, Helen thought.

She felt happy living with the Pettys. Sometimes the hours she worked were just as long as at Mrs Grice's, but it was different here. She liked the children and enjoyed running around after them more than doing housework. Of course there was housework, too – washing-up, ironing, socks and tea towels to be darned, as well as the cleaning – but Mrs Petty never worried if things didn't get done.

And Helen always had her free time to herself. Up in her room, where she was allowed candles and a hot-water bottle, she liked to lie on the bed and read. She read the books she had brought with her – *Heidi* and *Jane Eyre* – and Mrs Petty said she could borrow books from the living-room as long as she was careful with them. After a few weeks she began to feel like one of the family, and the farm on the hill faded in her imagination.

January went by, and most of February.

It was on a Wednesday evening towards the end of February that everything changed.

As usual Helen was helping Mrs Petty put the children to bed. They were washed and in their nightclothes and their father had been in to kiss them good night and had gone back to his newspaper.

Dennis, quiet at last, and smelling of talcum powder, was curled in his cot, his thumb resting against his lower lip. Irene padded about barefoot, delaying her own bedtime. She grasped the top bar of the cot and looked in. "He's away," she said, using her mother's phrase. "Mummy, I want Helen to read me my story tonight."

"You must get into bed first."

"I want to sit on Helen's lap."

"All right. If Helen doesn't mind."

Helen didn't. She liked the soft weight of Irene in her arms and the warm breath on her cheek. Irene clambered up, clutching *Hansel and Gretel*. Her mother kissed her good night and went out.

"I like it when you read," said Irene. "It makes sense. When Amy used to read to me the words were all muddled up. Helen, why did Amy go home to Church Sheldon?"

Helen stared at the open book without seeing it.

Church Sheldon.

That was the place. That was the name she had been waiting for. It had been there all the time in her memory, and now Irene had released it.

Church Sheldon was where she would find her father's home.

"Helen..." Irene was wriggling.

"I think she was homesick," said Helen. Her heart beat fast. "Irene, where *is* Church Sheldon? Do you know?"

"It's in the country." Irene twisted a strand of hair. "We went to the country once. It *smelled*." She wrinkled her nose and giggled.

"Is it far away – Church Sheldon?" Helen persisted.

"Mummy said it's near. She said, 'You can go home every week, Amy. It's no distance at all.'"

"On the bus?"

"On the train." Irene fidgeted. She had lost interest in Amy's problems. "Read to me, Helen."

Helen began: "'Once upon a time there was a poor woodcutter...'"

Irene lolled and put her thumb in her mouth.

It was nine o'clock before Helen was free to go up to her room and think.

CHAPTER NINE

The next day was Thursday, Helen's afternoon off. She whisked through her work and left the house promptly.

It was market day, and she could hear, across several streets, the sounds of the cattle auction. In the station forecourt she moved against the flow of people coming off a train: women with covered baskets, small children clinging, men and women with reddish, all-weather tans.

Some of these people must be from Church Sheldon, she thought. Perhaps one of them was John Davies. She looked at the faces of the men coming down the station steps, but there was no one who looked in the least like her father in that old photograph.

The timetables were ranged along the walls. At first she could not find Church Sheldon, and thought Irene must have been mistaken;

but then she discovered it, tucked away on a branch line going south. It was only two stops down the line, a twenty-minute journey. So near! She could go today.

But – what would she do when she got there? How would she find the farm? Who would she ask? And what would she say?

She realized for the first time that finding the town was only the beginning.

She hovered by the ticket booths, undecided. People bumped into her as they hurried by.

Her courage failed her.

I'll go on Sunday, she thought.

But she didn't. And when the following Thursday came around she put it off again. She was afraid. She didn't know what she would discover. And besides, she thought, suppose I do find my father, I can't just leave the children. It was Irene's birthday soon, and Helen was making her a doll's dress out of scraps she'd bought at the market.

I don't want to go, she realized. She pushed Church Sheldon to the back of her mind.

March the fourteenth was Irene's birthday – a Saturday. There was to be a family party: the grandparents were coming from Oswestry. Helen was kept busy the day before, washing up and running to the shops, while Mrs Petty cooked. She had finished the doll's dress the previous night, and wrapped it in a scrap of tissue paper, tied with ribbon. She gave it to Irene first thing on Saturday morning, and Irene hugged her and rushed to put it on the doll.

Later that morning Helen cleaned all the silver, ironed the tablecloth, and made tea when the visitors arrived. She whisked in and out of the living-room, scarcely noticed by the family, delivering tea and collecting empty cups while the adults chattered and the children shrieked and crawled about in the wrapping paper.

When one o'clock came she loaded up the trolley and served lunch. Afterwards she saw the grandmother jigging Dennis on her knee, the grandfather teasing Irene. She saw, too, the likeness between Irene and her grandfather.

"We're going out, Helen," Mrs Petty said. "Just down to the park to see the ducks."

And off they went, Dennis protesting against his reins, Irene clutching her doll in one hand and a bag of breadcrumbs in the other.

Helen was left with the washing-up and the silence.

They're a family, she thought. And I'm just a servant. I can never be anything else to them.

She knew then that she had to go to Church Sheldon and search for John Davies. She'd find the farm, and perhaps – it had happened before, to other people – she'd find her father alive; be a daughter, not a servant.

Tomorrow, she decided.

But on Sunday Mrs Petty said, "Helen, I hope you won't mind doing a bit of cleaning-up this morning. The house is in such a mess. I'll make your time up another day, of course."

"I – I was going out," said Helen. Now that she had made her decision she wanted to act immediately.

"Oh, you can have the rest of the day off. It's just an hour or two."

"But I need a day."

Mrs Petty paused then, and looked at her. "Are you going to Birmingham? I didn't think you had any family."

"I'm going to Church Sheldon." Suddenly she wanted to tell Mrs Petty, to share the weight of it all. For so long she had been alone, planning and searching, keeping her secrets. "I have to go. It's why I came to Hemsbury. To find my father."

"Your father?"

Mrs Petty stared. She picked up the kettle. "I'll make a cup of tea," she said, "and you'd better tell me all about it."

"But you don't know he's alive," said Mrs Petty. Helen had told her everything – except that she was only twelve. "It's more likely, I'm

74

afraid, that he died. Much more likely. You do understand that, don't you?"

Helen did, but she didn't accept it. She tried to sound grown-up and rational. "He must have had a family. I'll find *them*."

"But, my dear child," said Mrs Petty, "have you thought that they may not want you?"

"All the same, I want to meet them," said Helen obstinately.

Mrs Petty sighed. "And you say his name was Davies? It's a very common name. There must be dozens, even in the Sheldon area. You can't traipse around... I suppose there's the post office; you could ask there; or the shops... Didn't your mother ever try to find out if he had come back?"

"What do you mean?"

"Well, she might have written to the War Office, made enquiries, tried to find his family herself."

"I don't know." But Helen was sure her mother had not done any of those things. She wasn't much of a letter-writer, and she was frightened of authority; she would never have known how to "make enquiries". "She wasn't – you know – clever, like that," she explained, and felt ashamed, as if she had betrayed Mum.

"I'll tell you what we'll do," said Mrs Petty briskly, clearing away the tea cups. "You stay here and help me today, and then tomorrow –

oh, dear, tomorrow's washday, isn't it? – on Tuesday you can have the whole day off. It'll be better to go on a weekday. More trains for a start, and the shops will be open. You won't find anyone to ask on a Sunday."

Helen realized that was true.

"Take his photograph with you. And if you get any information, come straight back and tell me. You see, it might be better to write, in the first place. Mr Petty and I will help you. Is that agreed?"

And Helen, despite her overwhelming desire to be off at once, was obliged to say, "Yes. Thank you, Mrs Petty."

CHAPTER TEN

Helen went to Church Sheldon on the seventeenth of March. The weather had turned cold – "cold enough for snow," Mrs Petty said. "Now mind what I told you, Helen. Make enquiries and see if you can get an address to write to. Don't stay too long. Try and get the five o'clock train back."

Helen nodded. She hadn't been able to eat much breakfast. She put on her coat. In one of the pockets was her father's photograph and her purse with two shillings of her wages in it; in the other was a sandwich for her lunch wrapped in greaseproof paper.

Alone, at last, in the train, she leaned back in her seat and looked out of the window. The outskirts of town disappeared quickly, and were replaced by countryside. All around were bleak, bare fields, leafless trees, and, in the distance, hills.

There's nothing here, she thought. She had never seen anywhere so empty.

The train stopped at Tupley, where there seemed to be only three or four houses. An old man got off, carrying a string shopping bag, and shuffled away.

The train moved on. The hills were closer now. Deep valleys ran between them and there were patches of snow near their summits. Helen saw sheep gathered in knots under wind-bent hedges, narrow paths snaking across hillsides, tiny clusters of farm buildings. Perhaps one of them was her father's home.

Mrs Petty had said, "'Farmers' can mean different things, Helen. Landowners, with tenants. Or two goats on a smallholding. Or anything in between."

Helen had seen a grand country house standing on a rise above the railway line. She had a brief daydream of being an heiress, a rich man's long-lost daughter. But it seemed unlikely, and she wasn't even sure she would want it. One of those cottages that looked as if they had grown out of the hillside: that was where she expected to find him.

The train went into a cutting, and when it came out there were buildings: houses, a church, a schoolyard. They had arrived in Church Sheldon.

It was a little place, compared with Hemsbury: a few streets and a church in a circle of dark hills. She walked up the road from the station and found herself in the main shopping area.

Try the post office, Mrs Petty had said.

Helen passed a butcher's, a greengrocer's, a chemist's with glass jars in the window like those in Mr Petty's shop. At the top of the road was the market square. She looked around – noticed a bus stop and a war memorial.

The post office was on the next corner. The postmistress looked busy – too busy, surely, to bother with her. Helen walked off, down the street. When she came back, she saw through the window that the counter was free.

She paced up and down outside, reluctant, now, to go in and try to explain.

But I can't go home without trying, she thought.

She took the photograph out of her pocket and pushed open the door.

"Davies … that's a common name here," the postmistress said.

"It's John," said Helen. "John Edward Davies. He went missing in the war, but I don't know whether he came back." She brought out the photograph – the studio one of her father in his uniform.

The woman took it and looked, shaking her head. "I don't know him. But then he'd be older, could have changed a bit. Relation of yours, is he?"

Helen nodded. She could see that the woman was burning up with curiosity and would soon be telling other customers about the young Brummie girl who'd come asking questions; they'd all be speculating about her. She didn't like that, but it couldn't be helped. And besides, perhaps one of them would know something.

"You could look at the war memorial," the woman suggested.

The war memorial stood in the centre of the market square, surrounded by decaying wreaths and crosses. As she approached it and saw the lists of names – so many – a knot of fear gathered and tightened in her chest. If he's here, she thought, I don't want to know.

But she forced herself to look; walked round till she found the *D*s.

> PTE. A. R. DAVIES
> GUN. L. DAVIES
> PTE. G. A. DAVIES

Not there. Her heart beat fast. She felt strange, light-headed. Did that mean – it must mean, surely – that he *did* come back? He *was* alive?

Not knowing where best to try next, she chose

Cutler's, the chemist's, because it made her think of the Pettys. She caused an animated discussion.

"Now, wasn't Gerard Davies from Brook Farm reported missing?"

"Lost his leg, didn't he?"

The photograph was passed around. The women put their shopping bags down. Mrs Cutler leaned on the counter.

"No, that's not Gerard."

"Did Gerard have a brother?"

"Could it be one of Annie Davies' boys?"

"The middle one – Ewan?"

"John," said Helen. "His name's John."

"None of Annie's was called John."

"There's Martin Davies at Crowbank. He's got three sons."

"I think their name's Davey."

"What about those new people at Homerton? Aren't they Davies?"

"Not local, though, are they?"

They were enjoying the challenge, but Helen felt that she was getting nowhere. The photograph came back to her and she put it away.

"He lived on a hill," she said. "Under a hillfort."

"A hillfort?"

"A camp, is that?"

"She'll be meaning Belsmore Camp, I reckon."

"Or Norbury Rings?"

"Belsmore Camp is nearer."

The discussion took a new turn.

"You want to go to Belsmore, lass. There's three Sheldons, see: Church Sheldon, Little Sheldon and Sheldon-under-Belsmore."

"Sheldon-under-Belsmore," Helen repeated. It sounded like a charm; like "Open Sesame". "Where is it?" she asked.

"Not above two miles away."

"You can catch the bus," one of the women said. "The Tupley bus goes in ten minutes from Market Square – goes via Belsmore. You get the bus, you'll be there in no time."

Helen remembered, then, her mother saying that John had to catch a train from Hemsbury, and then a bus... Her excitement began to grow.

"There's only the one stop for Belsmore," another woman said. "Right by it you'll see there's a little post office and shop – in Mrs Roding's front room, it is. You ask there."

"I will," said Helen. "Thank you."

She sat on a mounting block near the bus stop in Market Square and ate her sandwiches. The bus was late. By the time it came she was tense, tight as a coiled spring. She felt sure that Sheldon-under-Belsmore was the place, that now she would find out everything; she would meet her father, find her home.

She had been on the bus barely ten minutes when the conductor said, "Here's

82

your stop, miss."

She got off, and the bus bumped away along the rutted road, leaving Helen in a village that seemed to consist of about a dozen houses, four of which were pubs and another a post office. Behind the houses the hill soared towards the ancient fort. She could just make out the shape of the turf banks. At the summit rocks broke the surface.

A track led up the hill. Was that the way? She turned towards the post office. A postman came out as she reached the door. He was carrying a bag of letters and heading for his bicycle, which was propped against the wall.

Helen approached him. "Excuse me, I'm looking for a farm." She took a breath. "Davies's farm. On the hill."

He looked surprised. "Davies's? You mean old Mrs Davies up at the Linstone?"

So it was there! She had found it! Helen let out her breath. Mrs Davies at the Linstone. This was the one. It had to be. "Is it up there?" She pointed.

"That's right. Near the top, just below Belsmore Camp." His expression was hopeful. "You going up there, by any chance?"

"Yes." Mrs Petty had said don't visit; write. But how could she wait, now? She had to go. She had to find out. "Yes. I'm going up. Is it far?"

"Oh, it's not too far, but it's steep. Hard on

the old knees. I've got a letter here for Mrs Davies. You wouldn't deliver it, I suppose?"

He pulled out the letter. Helen took it eagerly. It would give her an excuse to call.

"She doesn't get many letters, I'm glad to say," the postman said. "That'll be from her Margaret; it's got a Welsh postmark. She'll be glad to see that."

Helen wanted to say, "Does she have a son, too?" but couldn't bring herself to ask. Not now, when she was so near.

"Take the turning to the left," the postman said. "You'll see a farm there. That's Redfern's. Go past it, and keep on up the hill till you come to a big stone at the side of the path. Davies's is just by there, by the Linstone."

And a few minutes later Helen, with the letter in her hand, was walking along a frozen muddy lane that led up the hill towards the Linstone and Belsmore Camp.

At the bottom of the lane she passed Redfern's farm, where a chained dog barked, startling her. There were cows, too, in a yard deep in mud and manure. Helen wrinkled her nose at the smell. She had never seen cows close to before; she was glad they were behind a gate.

The track led on, and soon she found herself high above the village, climbing a steep grassy hillside scattered with pockets of snow. A bitter wind whipped her hair against her cheeks and made her eyes water. There were icy puddles on the track and clusters of tiny icicles hanging from grassblades. Frozen mud crunched under her shoes.

She saw sheep, and heard their voices carrying far across the valley. They had long dirty fleeces, and bits of grey wool were caught on the wire fence that bordered the path.

But there was no sign yet of the stone the postman had described. Helen paused, and squinted up at the hillside. It was so bare and wild – how could anyone live here? She began to feel overwhelmed by the emptiness.

She trudged on. High above her loomed the rocky crest of Belsmore Camp. A sheep crossed her path and Helen paused, nervous. But the sheep was scared of her; it skittered away.

And then she rounded a bend in the path and saw the Linstone – an ancient, weathered stone half-buried in the earth and leaning, like the stunted trees, as if from centuries of unremitting wind. Beyond it, tucked into a dip in the land and sheltered by a coppice, was a cluster of stone buildings: Davies's farm.

She felt suddenly afraid. This place was so strange. Mrs Petty was right. She should not have come without warning. What could the woman who lived here possibly want with her?

Loud barking erupted from the farmyard. A

dog rushed towards her.

Helen stood still in terror. The dog – a black and white collie – stopped too, and wagged its tail.

A woman came out of the house. She was old, thin, with scraped-back hair and a long dress with a dark apron over it. Her face was hollow-cheeked, tanned red by the wind.

Helen didn't want to meet her. She remembered Mrs Grice. I don't like old people, she thought.

"Here, Jess!" the woman called, and the dog bounded back to her side. She looked at Helen.

"Come up, lass. Don't be afraid."

Helen approached, wary of the dog, and held out the letter. "Mrs Davies? The postman asked me to bring this."

"Oh! Thank you." She glanced at the envelope and put it in her apron pocket, then turned her attention to Helen. "But you didn't come all the way up here to bring me a letter. I don't know you, do I?"

She spoke slowly, with a soft country accent, very different to the clipped city speech Helen was used to.

"I wanted to meet you," said Helen, "to ask you – " her heart was beating fast as she took out the photograph of her father – "to ask you if you know this man?"

Mrs Davies took the photograph. Helen saw her start. She looked up, frowned. Her expression was almost accusing. "Where did you get this?"

"From my mother. The man is my father," said Helen.

The woman stared. She seemed to grasp at the dog for support, curling her fingers in its fur. "Your father?"

"Yes."

"And – what is your name, lass?"

"Helen … Smith." As she said it Helen realized, for the first time, that if her parents had been married it would have been Helen Davies.

She saw the same realization in the woman's face, and saw that it was unwelcome. People didn't want to know about illegitimate children. Perhaps Mrs Davies would send her away.

"Helen Smith," the woman repeated. She put out a hand, gestured towards the door. "Well, Helen, you'd best come in. If Johnny's your father, then I must be your grandmother."

CHAPTER ELEVEN

Helen followed her into the house. The dog came, too; it wagged its tail and looked up at Helen with brown shining eyes.

"Take your coat off. Sit down," said Mrs Davies. (Helen could not think of her as "grandmother"). "I'll make tea."

She used a jug to ladle water from a bucket into the kettle, and stood the kettle on a trivet over the fire. Still with her back to Helen, and silent, she busied herself fetching cups and putting out squares of bread pudding on a plate. Helen realized that she was shocked and trying to assemble her thoughts before she spoke.

There was a wooden settle at the side of the fireplace. Helen sat down on the edge of it and clasped her hands tightly in her lap.

I'm not wanted here, she thought. She's asked me in to be polite, but she doesn't want me.

A black cat lay on a rug by the fire. It glared at her with yellow eyes as if it, too, resented her intrusion. Helen drew back her feet and tried to ignore it. She raised her eyes to the cluttered mantelpiece: candles, matches, tea caddy, clock, letter-rack. She noticed bunches of dried herbs and a side of bacon hanging from the ceiling beams, and a little row of books – the titles tantalizingly out of sight – on a shelf near the fireplace.

Mrs Davies put a small table by the fire, close to Helen, and set the tea things on it. She sat down in the chair opposite and the dog settled at her feet and put its nose between its paws. Helen felt a wariness emanating from the woman, almost a hostility. Mrs Davies was guarded, like the cat.

"Is my father alive?" Helen asked. She twisted her fingers in her lap.

Mrs Davies looked up. Her eyes, clear green, connected with Helen's. "Alive? Johnny? Oh, yes, he's alive, thank God."

Helen felt joy – a warm glow expanding inside her. It must have lit up her face, for Mrs Davies smiled, then, for the first time, and Helen knew there had been a breakthrough: they could talk about Johnny; he belonged to both of them. "Bless you, child," Mrs Davies exclaimed. "How long have you been searching for him? Were you told he was dead?"

"My mother... They said missing, presumed

dead…" Helen could scarcely speak; something hurt in her throat. "But I hoped…"

"He *was* missing a long time," said Mrs Davies, and the smile faded. "The waiting was terrible. My eldest son, George, was killed in 1915. And then two years later the telegram came saying Johnny was presumed…" She looked into Helen's face. "You're like him," she said. "I can see it now. And we never knew. *He* never knew. You're Alice's child, aren't you?"

Helen nodded. "She died. In November. They were going to send me to an orphanage…" Embarrassed, she felt her eyes swim with tears. "Is he here?"

"No. Not any more. He's a few miles away. He works on a big estate – has a cottage there. But he'll come. He'll want to meet *you* – I know he will." She shook her head, wonderingly. "You *are* like him. You must be twelve, thirteen now?"

"Twelve," said Helen. She knew there was no need to lie any more. "Thirteen in May."

Mrs Davies poured the tea, and passed Helen a cup. Helen fell silent. She was far away, with her father in his cottage, imagining their meeting, their happiness at finding each other, their new life together.

"Johnny loved your mother, Helen," Mrs Davies said. She got up, stretched slowly, easing the stiffness, and went into the next room. When she came back she was carrying an envelope. She took out a photograph. "He sent me this. About 1916, it would have been."

The photograph was new to Helen. It was a head and shoulders portrait of her mother, with some leafy bushes out of focus behind her. Her hair was pinned up in soft coils, and she looked much younger than Helen had ever seen or imagined her before. She was smiling, radiant, as if lit from within.

"She was such a pretty girl," said Mrs Davies. She sighed. "But I did think, then, 'She's a little thing – doesn't look strong; will she cope with life on a farm?' "

She'd have coped, Helen thought; Mum always coped – though the Mum she remembered was not this shining girl.

"He said he'd bring her home to meet me," her grandmother went on, "but it was difficult, with her being in service and him not getting leave often. I never did meet her."

The room had grown darker. Helen looked at the window and saw that it had begun to snow. Her grandmother had noticed, too. "Look at that weather! You wouldn't think it was March. I must feed the animals soon and get them shut away."

But Helen was thinking about her mother. "Why didn't he come back to her – to us?" she asked.

"Oh, Helen, he wanted to. You mustn't

think... He didn't desert your mother. Didn't mean to. He couldn't find her, you see. It was a year or more before he came out of hospital, longer than that before he could get about. He wrote to her, of course, but the letters were returned; she'd moved on. When he was well again he spent months searching, trying to find friends, people she'd worked with. I got angry with him – I'm sorry to say it. I thought he was wearing himself out, wasting himself. I wanted him to come home and settle down." She studied Helen again. "Born in May, you said. So it would have been about the time he went missing that she realized... Poor girl! She'd have been dismissed from her place. No wonder he never found her... Where are you living now, child? How did you get here?" She pushed the plate of bread pudding nearer to Helen. "Eat up."

Helen obliged. "Hemsbury," she said, between mouthfuls. "I'm working there as a maid."

"Working?"

Helen explained. She told her grandmother everything, from the moment when Mrs Bradley had decided to send her to the orphanage. Mrs Davies listened, nodding, sometimes shaking her head in amazement.

"I must tell Johnny," she said at last. "I'll send a letter tomorrow. Best if I do it soon, before he finds out through the grapevine."

"The grapevine?"

"Gossip. If you've been showing his photograph around town and asking about him..."

"But I never told anyone he was my father."

Mrs Davies burst out laughing. "You wouldn't need to, my love! Those women will have worked that out for themselves. No, the sooner I tell him the better. He hardly ever goes into Church Sheldon, but – " She checked herself as if about to say more, then went on briskly, "Best if he comes here. Let me see: it's Tuesday. Do you have Sunday off?"

"Yes."

"Come Sunday, then, for tea. Johnny will be free then. Yes. Best if you meet him here."

Again, Helen had the feeling of something withheld; but her grandmother's next words seemed to resolve it. "I must warn you, Helen, he was badly injured in the war. He's lame in his left leg. But that isn't all. It's his mind. He has nightmares. And he gets moods on him; his nerves..."

Helen adjusted her mental picture of her father; he appeared before her pale, leaning on crutches. She would take care of him.

Mrs Davies got up and fetched her coat. She pushed her feet into a pair of oversized boots that stood behind the door. "Put your coat on," she said. "Come and meet the animals."

She opened the door, and a flurry of snowflakes blew into the room. Helen was thrilled; she loved snow.

Mrs Davies led the way out. "Didn't expect this much snow – or so soon."

Helen and Jess followed her across the yard towards the outbuildings. Mrs Davies shouted over her shoulder, "You can't walk back to the village in this, girl. Not in those shoes. It's laying fast."

Helen hadn't even thought about getting back, but now she remembered. "I said I'd catch the five o'clock train."

"Don't worry. I'll take you to Church Sheldon in the cart." They had reached one of the wooden buildings. "Here's the stable." And with love in her voice she added, "And here's Megan."

Megan was a dark brown pony – a Welsh hill pony, Mrs Davies said. She came eagerly towards them, her breath hanging in clouds on the cold air.

Mrs Davies petted her, and put fresh hay into her manger. "She's an old lady, like me. Past her best, aren't you, Megan? But we suit each other. You can stroke her nose, Helen."

But Helen was frightened of the big plunging head and the way the lips curled back to reveal alarming teeth.

The nanny-goat seemed safer: small, except for her swollen belly. "She'll have her kids soon," said Mrs Davies. "You'd like them. Mind you, I prefer a cow, myself. A nice, sensible animal. You can have a conversation with a cow."

Helen sensed some loss. "Haven't you got one now?"

"I had to sell Dora. The year before last. Money was tight." Helen had noticed, as they went around, that the farm seemed to have shrunk: buildings stood empty, a door hung from its hinges; the frozen pond had a heap of corrugated iron and rusty tools dumped at its edge. She noticed, too, how stiffly her grandmother moved.

"Let's chase up these hens," the old woman said, "and shut them away for the night. Then we'll go and feed the sheep."

Chasing the chickens was fun. Helen was in fits of laughter as they scurried about in the flying snow, which was coming down thicker than ever.

"Look at the snow!" she exclaimed in delight, as her grandmother finally shut the hen-house door.

But Mrs Davies didn't share her enthusiasm. She got Helen to help her heave a bale of hay from the barn and put it into a handcart and push it out to the far field, directly below Belsmore Camp.

Jess padded at Helen's side, looking up at her and wagging her tail. Helen reached out cautiously and touched the dog's head. It felt sleek and warm. I like Jess, she thought.

Mrs Davies began to call, and Helen saw, through the snowstorm, a movement of animals down from the hill.

The sheep mobbed them as they entered the field, pushing and jostling, and running in front of them as they tried to pitch the hay into the cratches. And yet they were wild, too – not used to being handled, Mrs Davies said. They leapt away if Helen put out her hand. Some of them had lambs running beside them, and some were heavy with lambs still unborn.

Helen was not so frightened of the sheep as she had been of Megan, and she loved the lambs. She watched their tails wagging as they sucked.

"Won't they be cold, out in the snow?" she asked.

"No," said her grandmother. "They're hardy beasts. Better outside. Less likely to get sick. But I keep them in if they're a bit weak."

She led Helen back to the yard, to a shelter where a ewe and a lamb were penned. The lamb was curled up asleep in the hay.

Mrs Davies smiled. "He's not hers. He was an orphan and she'd lost her own lamb. Such a struggle I had to get her to accept him! Your father would have done better. He's got a way with animals, has Johnny."

Helen gazed at the lamb. She wanted to be like her father; *she* wanted to have a way with animals.

"You'd best get indoors," said her grandmother. "Those silly little shoes of yours are
soaked through. We'll dry them out before
you go. And we'll make plans."

CHAPTER TWELVE

Plans. Did that mean she'd soon be coming back here for good – that she wouldn't have to stay with the Pettys? Helen didn't dare ask. She remembered Mrs Bradley's words: "Even if we could trace your relatives, you would have no claim on them." It was all up to Mrs Davies now. And John, of course. Surely *he* would want her.

"Hang your wet coat there, Helen," said her grandmother. "And take your shoes off. We'll put newspaper in them and leave them to dry."

Helen padded across the tiles in her socks and looked out of the window. The snowflakes were bigger now and falling faster than ever. She could see a deep drift forming against the stable door.

Mrs Davies came and stood beside her. "You know, I doubt Megan'll get through to Sheldon. I reckon you'll have to stay the night."

Helen was alarmed. "Mrs Petty will be worried!"

"It can't be helped. She'll guess what's happened."

"I suppose so." But Helen still felt anxious.

"Come and see your room," her grandmother said.

The house was single-storey, with a loft reached by a ladder. Helen hoped she could sleep up there, but Mrs Davies said, "I don't use the loft much these days," and led her to a bedroom downstairs. It contained two single beds and, in one corner, a carved wooden cradle. There was a washstand, a mirror, a worn rug on the floor. The room was as simple as a maid's, yet different: the red eiderdown looked cosy; there was a row of books on a shelf; and there were pictures on the walls – one of a girl in old-fashioned clothes selling flowers, another of the Good Shepherd carrying his lost lamb.

"I like the Good Shepherd," said Helen.

"Margaret liked that one, too."

Helen looked at the books: two old annuals, *The Big Book of Make and Do; Robin Hood.* "Was this Margaret's room?"

"All the children have slept here at different times. I remember George used to line up his toy soldiers along that wall – and woe betide me if I moved them! And Johnny always wanted his bed under the window; so he could

99

lean out and touch the grass, he said. See, the land slopes up behind the house." Helen went to the window. Snow had settled on the outside sill, a crooked line, higher in one corner. The cold outside made the room seem warm.

Mrs Davies pulled back the eiderdown and felt the blankets. "I'll air these. And find some sheets."

Helen turned to her in alarm. "I haven't got a nightie!"

Her grandmother smiled. "I can lend you one."

She began stripping the bed. Helen helped her.

"We've had some snowstorms here in our time," Mrs Davies said. "I remember once it was so deep it covered that window. We had to dig a passage through it to the outhouses. And the cat went out and walked about on top of the snow. George made a sledge, that winter, for moving the animals' feed –"

"Oh!" exclaimed Helen. "A sledge!"

Sledging was one of the many things she had dreamed of doing but which had never been possible in her other life. She turned eagerly to her grandmother with the question that was uppermost in her mind. "Mrs Davies –"

"Gran. You'd best call me Gran."

"Gran, I will be able to live with my father, won't I? You won't send me back?"

"I won't send you back."

Helen smiled, and felt tears coming too.

Her grandmother continued. "I'm sure you'll be able to live with your father, and if, for any reason, you don't want to –"

"Oh, but I *will* want to! I will."

How could she possibly not want to? Perhaps because of his bad leg – or the moods Gran had spoken of. But I won't mind that, Helen thought. I'll understand. I'll take care of him. She saw the two of them together, sitting by the fire while the snow fell outside, perhaps with a dog – yes, a dog like Jess.

"Has he got a dog?" she asked.

"What? Oh, yes, Johnny always has a dog. Bob, he's got now. Good little fellow, Bob."

In her imagination Helen patted Bob, who dozed at John's feet. "I *will* want to live there," she insisted.

"Well, if you don't, if you change your mind – there's always a home for you here. Is that understood? You need never be a servant again, unless you want to."

Helen wanted to hug her grandmother, but they were halfway through folding up a blanket and anyway Gran didn't look a hugging sort of person. "You said we'd make plans," she reminded her.

"Well, you *will* have to go back, first, and explain to Mrs Petty. She might want you to work out your notice, although, as you're under age…"

Helen didn't want to think about that. She dreaded explaining to Mrs Petty how she'd lied about her age and ignored her instructions about coming straight back.

They hung the sheets and blankets on a rack by the fire. The light was fading. Gran lit an oil lamp and placed it in the centre of the kitchen table. Its bright glow made the shadows deeper in the corners of the room and darkened the sky outside.

Helen went to the window and watched the snowflakes tumbling down. Somewhere out there was her father's home.

"Where does he live?" she asked.

"You'll be able to see it in the morning from that window. There's a gap between the hills, and you can see Church Sheldon. Rowton Hall stands in the fields on the far side. John works there – does a bit of gardening, odd jobs and the like." She shook her head, disapproving. "He should be running a farm. Livestock, that's his calling."

Helen wanted to ask why he didn't help run *this* farm, but her grandmother said, "Well, if you're not going back to Hemsbury you'll want some supper. Will bread and cheese suit you? And the rest of the bread pudding?"

After supper Gran got out an album of photographs. "There's your grandfather. He died ten years ago. I don't think he ever recovered from George's death… Oh, here we are on our wedding day. Look at my mother, in her button boots that she kept for best, and Dad with his high collar. And here are the children: George, Margaret, John."

She turned the pages back, to a pencil sketch of a girl in a long, full-skirted dress and a white apron and cap. "That's me. My brother drew it. I was nineteen then – in service at Rushbrook."

"You were in service, too?"

"Oh, yes. There were six of us at home and I was the eldest, eating my mother out of house and home, I daresay. Any road, she says to me, 'You'll be eleven in September, Lizzie; it's time we found you a place.' And I was packed off to a big house the other side of Belsmore to work as a kitchen-maid. Eighteen sixty-nine, that would have been. August."

"You were eleven?" exclaimed Helen.

"Yes. Nearly eleven. I stayed a year. Hated it. I had to be up at four to scrub out the dairy and help with the churning, and I never got to bed till nine. I've worked as hard since, but it's different when it's your own farm. And you see, the worst thing, then, was missing my brothers and sisters. There was no fun."

Helen wondered what it would be like to have brothers and sisters. She thought of all those children at school, pushing, asserting themselves, and was not sure she would like it.

And yet she liked Irene and Dennis...

There were more photographs at the end of the book, but Gran didn't show them to Helen. She shut the album and said, "Those sheets and blankets will be aired now. Why don't you go and make up your bed while I read Margaret's letter? I'd forgotten all about it. And later, when you're asleep, I'll write to John."

"Is his house like this one?"

"Not so different."

But once again Helen had the feeling that there was something her grandmother wasn't telling her. What could it be? *Was* it about his injuries? She gnawed at a fingernail, the one she always bit the most. "Gran, he will want me, won't he – my father?"

"I know he'll want you," said her grandmother, and this time there was nothing hidden.

Next morning Helen woke to cold white light and the hush of snow. She shivered. Last night Gran had heated a brick in the oven and wrapped it in an old vest to warm the bed, but it had long since lost its heat.

She dressed under the covers, then got out of bed and opened the curtains. The snowfall had stopped. A white hillside rose in front of the window. She squatted down so that her head was level with the sill and saw Belsmore

Camp on the skyline.

From the other side of the house she could hear the scrape of a shovel. She went out into the yard. The sun was shining. The air was blue and clear and the snow sparkled.

She looked for the gap between the hills that Gran had told her about. There it was: and she could see Church Sheldon with the snow on its roofs and beyond it, in the distant white fields, a big house standing alone. Rowton Hall. Her father was there, in a cottage somewhere in the grounds. So near, and she couldn't reach him. If I were a bird, she thought, I'd fly straight there.

Gran had cleared a path to the barn and was hauling bales of hay onto the sledge and tying them in place.

"Wait!" said Helen. "I'll help!"

"Get some boots on, then," said Gran. "Look in the cellar, behind the door."

Helen found a pair of boots – old and split, but they'd do. She ran outside.

"It's a big job, feeding the animals in bad weather," said Gran.

"You ought to have help. Why doesn't my father live here?"

"Oh – there are reasons," said Gran. Secrets again. Helen felt frustrated.

"I get a man in for shearing," said Gran. "And Redferns – they've got the farm at the bottom of the lane – they'll always give a hand if I need."

"This place was bigger once, wasn't it?"

"It was. Right, help me pull the sledge now, will you? Yes, we had a lot more stock in the old days. But I can't manage it now." A thought seemed to strike her. "You'll have to go to school. At Church Sheldon."

"School?" Helen remembered her school in Birmingham – those hateful girls. Somehow, in escaping the orphanage she'd thought she'd escaped school, too.

"You shouldn't be working. You should have another year or more at school."

"I won't know anyone." She imagined them: big, rosy-faced bullies, with their country accents and knowledge, jeering at her.

"You'll get to know them."

But Helen didn't want to think about school. It was her father she was concerned with. Her father, and his home, and how soon she could go there and live with him.

The thaw began around midday. In the late afternoon Helen was sitting at the kitchen table, writing. She had discovered some coloured pencils in a drawer in her bedroom. "Those must be Johnny's," Gran had said. And she had given Helen paper – opened-out envelopes – to draw on. Helen started by drawing a tree, and then began to write, turning it into a family tree:

George Davies m. Elizabeth – ("What was

your name, Gran, before you were married?"
"Jebb," said Gran. "Elizabeth Jebb, born
1858 at High Farm, Tupley.") Helen wrote
that down, and added the children: George,
Margaret, John. With Gran's help, she put
in Margaret's husband and their four
children, and then herself. She wrote her
mother's name next to John's, but missed out
the "m." for "married".

Gran came and put a hand on her shoulder.
"We should be able to get down to the station
tomorrow."

Helen looked up. "Gran!" She'd had an
idea – a wonderful, simple idea. "Gran, if that
place is near, where my father lives, why don't
we go there, on the way to the station? We
could tell him, and –"

She saw her grandmother shaking her head.
"He'll be at work. He couldn't stop and talk.
And it'd be a shock."

"But I don't want to leave without even
seeing his home! Can't we just drive past?"

"No," said Gran, and her voice was so firm
that Helen knew there could be no argument.
"No. I've written to him. I'll put the letter in
the post. He can come on Sunday, and you can
meet him here. But before that we must settle
things with Mrs Petty."

Helen stiffened.

"You won't need to say anything," Gran
continued. "I'll explain."

"You'll come with me?"

Helen was scarcely able to believe what she had heard. A great weight was lifted from her. She was no longer alone.

"Of course I will," said Gran. "What did you expect? You're my granddaughter. Of course I'll come. And I'll explain everything."

"Everything? About the snow? About me not being fourteen?"

"Everything," said Gran. She looked out, at the darkening sky. "But right now we'd better shut those hens away."

Helen jumped up. "I'll do it."

The hens were difficult; they knew Helen wasn't the boss. But she would not call Gran; she persisted until they were all in.

She shut the door on them, satisfied. Far below she heard the sound of church bells and saw lights coming on, one by one, in the valley. The air was cold and clean, and a great stillness, such as she had never experienced before, lay over the farmhouse and its outbuildings and the surrounding countryside. In the paddock, half visible in the fading light, Megan grazed with a soft tearing sound; the hens grumbled to one another in their coop.

I wish Mum were here, Helen thought. If she hadn't died we could have come here together, and found Gran, and Mum and Johnny could have got married at last.

But even as she imagined it, she knew it

108

would not have happened. If Mum had lived they would never have come looking for John Davies. They would never have left the city. Helen remembered the view from their attic room in Hartland Road, that green hill. Mum had never taken her there, though it could not have been so very far away. Alice Smith, foundling, parents unknown, had accepted her lot in life; she didn't hope for or expect anything better.

But I do, Helen thought. She put aside her vague worries about whatever it was that Gran wasn't telling her. She had found her father, and she was going to live with him.

CHAPTER THIRTEEN

On Thursday morning Helen was woken by the flump of snow falling from the roof. The gutters dripped, and when she looked out she saw that the hillside was a messy patchwork of green and greyish white.

Back to Hemsbury, she thought.

Gran put on a brown dress with a cream lace collar (Helen guessed it was a best dress from long ago) and a round brooch at the neck, and polished lace-up shoes. She twisted her hair into a coil and pinned it. "There! That should be respectable enough for your Mrs Petty."

Under Gran's direction, Helen ironed her dress and cleaned her shoes. Cleaning her shoes was pointless, she thought, since the yard was deep in mud and slush, but she didn't say so.

Gran looked her over. "Your cardigan's a bit short in the sleeve."

"I've got a new one," said Helen. "Well, nearly. Mum was knitting it. There's only the button band to do, but I'm not very good at button bands; they go wavy."

"You need to stretch it as you sew it on," said Gran. "I'll show you."

Helen smiled. She felt cared for, in a way she had not felt since Mum died. Gran would help her with her knitting. Gran would come with her to Hemsbury.

When they boarded the train at Church Sheldon she sat and gazed at her grandmother, at the rough hands holding a pair of worn leather gloves, the face that was already trusted and familiar. She wanted to turn to everyone and tell them, "This is my gran!"

"It's a relief to see you, Helen," said Mrs Petty. She had telephoned the post offices at Sheldon and Belsmore on Wednesday morning, and discovered that Helen had gone up to the farm. "And now it seems you're only twelve years old! I should never have let you go if I'd known. But I'm glad you've found your family."

Gran explained about John. "I want him to meet Helen on Sunday. But she must spend the next few days working for you. That's only right: make up for those lost days, and give you time to advertise for a new girl."

"I must admit, I'd begun asking around

already," said Mrs Petty.

And Helen knew, then, that she would not regret leaving the Pettys, despite their kindness; to them she had only been a servant, after all.

Gran went home, and Helen's life returned to normal. Except that nothing was the same. All she could think about was the coming Sunday afternoon. She cleared ash, laid fires, carried water, played with the children, and through it all ran a golden thread: on Sunday I'm going to meet my father.

When Sunday morning came she felt sick with anticipation and couldn't eat her breakfast, even after an hour or more spent scrubbing the front step and cleaning the kitchen.

At last it was time to go. She went to her room and changed out of her mother's uniform into her own blue dress and cardigan. She took the pins out of her hair and let it fall back into its childish bob. She put on her coat and the red scarf and gloves.

"I'm sorry to lose you," said Mrs Petty. "And so are the children."

But Helen knew she had put an advertisement in the *Hemsbury Chronicle*. They would soon replace her.

"Goodbye," she said. "And thank you."

On the train once more, but this time with all her belongings beside her in two bags, Helen began to feel nervous. Now that the moment was almost upon her she felt an urge to hold back.

But when she arrived at Church Sheldon station there was her grandmother, waiting, in the cart, and Jess on the seat beside her.

"Gran!" she exclaimed.

All her reservations left her, and she ran towards them.

Jess bounded out of the cart and jumped up at Helen, leaving muddy paw-prints on her coat.

"She remembers you," said Gran. "Up you come. Sit here. Move over, Jess." She hesitated, then kissed Helen's cheek. "He's there," she said. "At the house."

Helen felt unable to speak. She watched the rise and fall of Megan's haunches as they drove along the road to Sheldon-under-Belsmore and took the turning up to the Linstone. The crest of Belsmore Camp came into view, and then the farm. She gripped the edge of the seat.

A man stood in the yard, watching them.

He was tall, thin, his face shaded by a cap and a coat collar pulled up high against the cold.

Mrs Davies guided the cart into the yard and the man seized Megan's bridle and patted her. Helen noticed his limp as he came to help them both down – first his mother, then Helen.

"Helen," he said, still holding her by her arms. They stared at each other. Helen saw an older man than she had imagined – older, and hurt. The left side of his face was scarred, and the scars had puckered so that his mouth had a slight twist to it.

He was studying her. Looking for my mother, Helen thought. And then he clutched her to him, and held her tightly, and she felt the rough cloth of his coat and smelt his tobacco. A button pressed into her cheek.

When he let her go he said, "Helen, I'm glad you're here. I want to know everything about you … about your mother … how you came to find us…" He spoke with a country accent, subtly different to Gran's, changed by his travels and the people he'd met.

"You'd best come inside, then, John," Gran said. "The child's cold."

She led the way in.

The kitchen smelled wonderfully of baking. Helen noticed scones cooling on a rack, and something that looked like ginger cake, and jam in a glass dish.

Her grandmother made tea. Then she said, "I need to see to the animals. I'll take Jess and leave you two to talk."

When she had gone Helen said, "I like Jess. I was frightened of her at first. But I like her now." She stopped, suddenly shy.

"I was frightened when I first went to the

city," said her father. "All that traffic, and noise, and smoke. I didn't know how to cross the road."

Helen laughed.

"You look like your mother when you laugh," he said. "Helen Alice. That's what she called you, isn't it? Your gran told me."

"She wanted me to have two names. She only had one herself because she was a foundling."

"Helen, tell me about Alice – about your mother. I want to know all about your life together."

Helen began to talk. She showed him the package of photographs and certificates and told him about her search. She talked about everything: Hartland Road, and the people there, her vague memories of the place before, her feelings about school, the way she had always had to keep quiet and still –

"We'll change all that," he said. "You'll be able to run about and make as much noise as you want."

Helen laughed. "But I don't want!" She told him about Jack, who had called her Mouse.

"It'll be different," he said. "You'll see." He smiled. "I don't earn much money, mind. Can't offer you riches. I went on a re-training scheme after the war: boot and shoe mending. Tried it for a while but it didn't work out. I'm back on the land now, gardening. You know I would have married your mother, Helen?"

"Gran told me."

He picked up the photograph of himself and Alice. "Phil Rankin took that. My friend who lived in Birmingham. He was killed in July that year. Helen, I searched for your mother for a long time; I was determined to find her. Of course, I didn't know about you. But you will stay with me now, won't you?"

The fire was bright; Helen felt as if its warmth came from inside her. She had found her father. He wanted her to live with him. They would be together, the two of them, as she and Mum had been together.

"It's not a big place, the cottage," her father said (and Helen heard the anxiety in his voice and silently reassured him: I don't care; it doesn't matter; we'll be happy), "but there's room for you, if that's what you'd like." He hesitated, then went on in a rush. "We talked about it last night. We want you to come and—"

"We?" said Helen. The fire within her went cold.

He put out a hand. "I'm married, Helen. I should have told you before, but I wanted us to talk first."

Helen sprang to her feet, knocking his hand aside. Married. How could he be married? "You said you loved my mother!"

"I did, Helen, but I lost her. I married Eva.

We have children – three of them –"

"No!" said Helen. She stepped back. Children! *She* was his child. He was *her* father.

He stood up too. "My family – they all want to meet you, Helen. They're quite excited about it. I brought this." He took a photograph out of his pocket, tried to show it to her. "Here's Eva. And this is Michael…"

Helen wouldn't look or listen. She backed away, her hands over her ears, shaking her head. "No!" she shouted. Her voice grew louder. "No! No! No! No!"

He caught her shoulders. "Helen, please! Don't get upset."

She pushed him off, still shouting. The voice seemed to come from somewhere else. She darted across the room, seized her coat from a chair, and ran outside.

CHAPTER FOURTEEN

Across the yard. Out through the gate.

"Helen!" her father pleaded. "Come back!"

But she ignored him. She had to get away, right away, away from everyone.

She began to climb.

They tried to follow her. She heard their voices caught and carried off on the wind. Then silence. She climbed on, up the hill, and despair folded itself around her.

Tears were streaming down her face. Her throat hurt. Her chest hurt. It was as if all the tears and shouting that had never happened at Hartland Road had come to overwhelm her now.

The wind caught her on the next bend, slapping her hair against her face.

A wife. Children.

She wouldn't share him. He was *her* father, not theirs. *Her* mother was the one he should have married. The picture she had built up of the two of them, together at last, sharing Mum's memory, was broken. He'd cheated her. He'd lied. He'd never meant to marry her mother – never searched for her. Helen's brief glimpse of the photograph had shown her three children. The eldest, a boy, looked eleven years old at least; her father had soon replaced Alice. There was a girl, too. A little girl. His daughter.

The way up grew steeper. She struggled against the wind, fought it. Her tears blinded her, and she lost the path, but still she kept moving up, towards the summit. Rocks broke the surface of the hillside. She passed into the lee of one big outcrop and the wind was abruptly cut off. The silence rang. She became aware of her cold hands and stinging face. She stepped out again and the force of the wind made her stagger.

She could see the hillfort above her now – the place she had imagined so often. But it was not a green hill; it was a desolation of wind and stone. The wind was so strong that she could not stand against it. She climbed back down to the safety of her sheltering rock. There she crouched and let the tears dry on her face and felt her resolution harden; she would not go back to the house, she would not live with his family, she would not share him.

Ages later, it seemed, she heard snuffling

and felt a lick on her cheek.

"Jess!" she exclaimed, and hugged the dog, burying her face in the warm fur. "Oh, Jess!"

Jess, all a-quiver, gave her a few more licks, then slithered out of her arms, bounded down the slope and disappeared around a bend in the path.

Helen felt bereft. "Jess! Where are you?" She staggered to her feet, stiff and cold.

And then Jess was back, and behind her a figure. For a moment Helen thought it was her father, and drew in her breath to protest; but no, it was her grandmother, bundled up in a man's greatcoat and with a scarf tied around her head.

She regarded Helen. "Are you going to stay there all night?"

Helen shook her head.

"Then you'd best follow me down."

Jess scurried between the two of them as they made their way back.

"Johnny's gone home," said Gran, over her shoulder.

Helen felt a pang mixed with relief.

They went into the house together. Gran filled the kettle for tea. Helen stood by the fire warming her hands with her back to the room.

"Are you hungry?" asked her grandmother.

"Yes," murmured Helen. She felt overwhelmed with shame at her outburst and that stupid flight up the hill.

And now, turning round, she saw that her grandmother was laying out tea on the table. There was a pretty cloth, embroidered with flowers in the corners, and little sandwiches, and scones, and jam – the feast she had prepared to share with her son and granddaughter: a celebration tea, all spoiled now.

Helen began to cry. "I'm sorry," she said. "I'm so sorry."

Her grandmother put her arms round her while she sobbed, muffling her face in the flour-dusted apron.

At last Helen drew back, swallowing tears; her throat jumped as she tried to speak. "The tea – all that work you did."

"We can eat it!"

"But I – I made him go."

"No, love, you didn't. *I* did. 'Leave her with me,' I said. 'Let her get used to the idea in her own time.' He's not angry with you, Helen – no one is. He'll come back."

"Why? He doesn't need *me*."

"Of course he does. You're his child – same as the others. He wants to take care of you."

Helen wiped her hand across her eyes. "Why didn't you tell me?"

Her grandmother considered. "Maybe I should have. But I thought, it's for Johnny to tell her, not me. I didn't want to scare you off – make you think he wouldn't want you. And, you see, I wanted to give Johnny time to talk to Eva about you."

Eva, thought Helen. He loves Eva, not my mum.

"That boy," she said, "in the photo he showed me. He looks nearly as old as me."

"He's older," said her grandmother.

Helen stared, bewildered.

"Michael is fourteen. But he's not your father's son. Eva was a widow when Johnny married her. Michael is Eva's son."

She went into her bedroom. When she came out she was holding a copy of the same photograph in a silver frame.

This time Helen looked.

Eva was a short, square-faced person with light-coloured bushy hair who smiled straight at the camera. She wore a lace blouse with a little round collar and a locket on a chain.

The two youngest children were like her.

"This is William," said Mrs Davies. "He's seven, soon be eight. And this is Patricia. We call her Patty."

Helen heard her grandmother's voice soften as she said the name; Patty's her favourite, she thought jealously.

"I don't want to live with them," she said.

"Well," said her grandmother, "you don't have to. Remember what I said? You could stay here."

Helen thought of the spare bedroom where she had spent two nights. She imagined her own things scattered about: her books, and hairbrush, her nightdress on the bed. She liked being here with Gran and Jess. But it wasn't what she'd set her heart on; it was second best.

"Stay a while," advised Gran. "You can change your mind any time. I won't be offended." She paused, and went on. "You'll have to meet them, though, before long. They're my family."

Helen picked at a loose thread on a cushion. "I wish he hadn't married Eva. He should have married my mum."

"We have to make the best of things the way they are," said her grandmother, and Helen guessed she was thinking of George, who had not come home from the war. "Just be glad you're here – that you were born."

Helen thought about what she had brought on herself. A family. Brothers. A sister – the word made her flinch; half-sister, she amended.

A stepmother.

She felt safer with Gran – for now, at least. "I'll stay," she said.

CHAPTER FIFTEEN

Helen jumped the stream, missed her footing, and slipped on the wet stones into the water. It didn't matter. She wore sturdy boots now, old-fashioned ones, bought by Gran at Sheldon market.

The stream was fast here, bubbling over stones. You could hear its clatter from the house. On the other side was a patch of woodland. Helen was looking for morning sticks, as Gran called them – kindling to light the fire. She broke the twigs and branches into manageable lengths and bundled them up in her apron. There were primroses growing at the edge of the wood. She picked some, and tucked them into her pocket. Gran would like to see them in a vase on the dinner table.

She climbed back up the slope to the house.

Gran was cooking, getting ready for the family; they were all coming today for Sunday dinner, and Gran had a chicken in the oven and potatoes ready for roasting, and spring cabbage from the garden. It was to be the first time the family had visited since Helen's arrival more than two weeks ago.

Gran was flustered. "Have you fed Megan?"

"Yes."

"And the chickens?"

"You know I have! And I've collected the eggs; they're in the bowl."

"Good girl. What do you think about a pudding? I could do a steamed one? Or there's bottled plums ... a plum tart?"

"With a lattice top?" said Helen. "Mum used to do that."

"Your mum!" said Gran. "She'll take some living up to." But she smiled.

It's because of me, Helen thought, me meeting her family; that's why she's in a tizzy. She felt strange herself – nervous. She looked for something to do, to take her mind off it. "Do you want some logs splitting?" It still amazed and delighted her that Gran let her use the axe.

"No. Tomorrow will do. But you could fetch water."

Helen took the pails and went down to the spring. It was half a mile from the house, but she didn't mind. She'd carried enough water since leaving Hartland Road, and resented it, but this was different. This was water for her and Gran and the animals: she was part of this place, not a servant. She didn't feel like a skivvy when she fetched it.

"How did I manage without you?" Gran had asked, the other day.

But Helen understood, now, why her father didn't live at the farm. "The time might come," said Gran, "when I'll get too old and have to go down the hill…" Her face clouded, and Helen knew she was thinking of the work-house. "But until then… Well, two women in a kitchen – it never works out."

"Don't you like Eva?"

"I like her well enough. She's a town girl, comes from down south, has different ideas – but we get on. You will, too."

But Helen wondered.

She took the pails of water into the house. Gran said, "Thanks, love. Now you run and play. Let me do this."

Helen called Jess, and climbed up to Belsmore Camp. It was her favourite place now. She loved the wide space open to the sky, the buffeting of the wind. She would patrol the banks with Jess, imagining that she was an Ancient Briton, on lookout for strangers.

And today she saw them. She looked down to the valley and saw them coming: her father and his family. She knew at once it was them: a horse and cart slowly moving along the road from Church Sheldon. The children in the cart were not visible, but she recognized the figure of her father driving, and beside him a woman – her stepmother.

Helen had a lookout post – a rock she liked to climb. She clambered to the top, stood up, and caught the shock of the wind. Strings of hair whipped her face, and her dress flattened itself against her legs. From here she could look down on the farm and see its smallness in the sweep of hills. From here, too, she could see Rowton Hall, where her father lived – where he wanted her to come and be part of his family.

The horse and cart must have reached the turning up to the Linstone, for it had disappeared from view behind Redferns'. Soon she would see it come round the corner and into the farm yard.

Jess heard them first. She barked. Helen saw the small figure of her grandmother come out of the house, and then the horse and cart was there at the gate, and her father climbed down and held the horse's bridle as Eva descended.

Helen heard their voices, cries of delight, and saw the little ones lifted down. Gran looked up towards her on her rock and signalled.

Jess deserted Helen. She leapt down and raced towards the group.

"Jess!" Helen cried in dismay.

The dog looked back, wagged her tail, but

continued her downward flight. Helen saw a dark-haired boy – Michael, it must be – meet Jess and receive her leaping embrace. Two small children ran to join in fussing the dog.

They *are* my family, Helen realized. All of them. I can't have Jess and Gran and not have them.

The little girl looked about the same age as Irene. She had spotted Helen on her rock and was pointing her out to the others.

But they were going inside. Gran went in, followed by Eva, and the two boys. Helen saw John glance up at her, then turn towards the house. He was holding Patty's hand, but Patty – her little sister Patty – tugged and twisted round and shouted something, waving to Helen.

She wants me to come too, Helen thought.

Their father ducked his head under the lintel.

"Wait!" shouted Helen.

She scrambled down from her rock. The wind caught her voice and blew it away and she had to shout louder still, "Dad! Patty! Wait for me! I'm coming down!"